D0846405

Savage Storms 2

Meesha

Lock Down Publications and Ca$h
Presents
Savage Storms 2
A Novel by *Meesha*

Meesha

Lock Down Publications
Po Box 944
Stockbridge, Ga 30281

Visit our website @
www.lockdownpublications.com

Copyright 2021 by Meesha
Savage Storms 2

All rights reserved. No part of this book may be reproduced in any form or by electronic or mechanical means, including information storage and retrieval systems without permission in writing from the publisher, except by a reviewer who may quote brief passages in review.
First Edition February 2021
Printed in the United States of America

This is a work of fiction. Names, characters, places, and incidents either are products of the author's imagination or are used fictitiously. Any similarity to actual events or locales or persons, living or dead, is entirely coincidental.

Lock Down Publications
Like our page on Facebook: Lock Down Publications @
www.facebook.com/lockdownpublications.ldp
Cover design and layout by: **Dynasty Cover Me**
Book interior design by: **Shawn Walker**
Edited by: **Kiera Northington**

Stay Connected with Us!

Text **LOCKDOWN** to 22828 to stay up-to-date with new releases, sneak peaks, contests and more...
Thank you.

Submission Guideline.

Submit the first three chapters of your completed manuscript to ldpsubmissions@gmail.com, subject line: Your book's title. The manuscript must be in a .doc file and sent as an attachment. Document should be in Times New Roman, double spaced and in size 12 font. Also, provide your synopsis and full contact information. If sending multiple submissions, they must each be in a separate email.

Have a story but no way to send it electronically? You can still submit to LDP/Ca$h Presents. Send in the first three chapters, written or typed, of your completed manuscript to:

LDP: Submissions Dept
Po Box 944
Stockbridge, Ga 30281

DO NOT send original manuscript. Must be a duplicate.

Provide your synopsis and a cover letter containing your full contact information.

Thanks for considering LDP and Ca$h Presents.

This book is dedicated to the Boss of all Bosses…

Eboneé Marie Abby
12/04/1984 - 10/24/2020

Eboneé, I miss you every day. The day I received the call that you passed was the day my heart was split in two. I went into a very dark place, because I couldn't believe you were no longer on this earth with me and many others. During that time, I was not happy at all. The one person I could always reach out to when I needed to talk, had been taken away from me. It took weeks for me to realize that you were still with me every step of the way. You made your presence known and got me right. Your words resonate in my mind daily and I smile every time I hear your voice. Keep pushing me forward. Your legacy will live forever and I'm going to do my part to make sure you're never forgotten. I'm thankful to have been able to bond with you and gave you your flowers before you made your transition. I love you, sis (you know we called each other that in private, lol) and oh how I would love to hear you say "love you more" one more time. But I'm sure I'll hear it more times than I want in the days to come. Fly high, baby. I know you're still running the show from afar.

#LongLiveThaBoss

Meesha

Chapter 1

Nicassy

When the door slammed behind Stone, I fell upon the bed and cried like a baby. In my mind, I was beating myself up because I should've kept my mouth shut, and kept living the life I'd developed with the man I'd grown to love. But, being the woman I was, I couldn't continue living a lie. Thinking Stone would brush off the way we met was stupid on my part, because Scony had already told me what he would've done had he been placed in that predicament.

Wiping my eyes, I walked to the closet and shuffled through the many designer clothes Stone had either given me money to purchase, or brought home just because. I had brought very little along with me when I came to Houston. Hell, I was only supposed to be in town to complete the job I never even attempted to go through with, after Stone took the bait.

The air in the bedroom felt thick and the quiet was deafening. I grabbed my phone from the nightstand and decided to call Kenzie and apologize for being the jealous friend I was for no reason. Being so close to death had me wanting to make things right between the two of us. My hands shook as I scrolled through my contacts, looking for Kenzie's name. It had been so long since I'd willingly called her and I felt bad that I'd erased her number from my memory. After hitting the call button, I listened as the phone rang several times. As I was about to end the call, Kenzie's voice filled my eardrums.

"Hello." I couldn't open my mouth to say hello in return. Instead, I sobbed lowly into the phone. "Nicassy! What's wrong with you?" Kenzie asked in an alarming voice.

"Kenzie, I'm so sorry," was the first thing to fall from my lips. I knew I would have to come better than that, because it wouldn't be enough when it came to Kenzie.

"What are you sorry for?"

"I've kept my distance from you for my own selfish reasons," I said, wiping at my eyes. "You have always been there for me no matter what, and I let my insecurities get in the way of our relationship. Will you forgive me, Kenzie?"

"There's nothing for me to forgive. You should be asking yourself for forgiveness because you were the one with the problem. You never told me what was on your mind, remember? The animosity was solely on your end, Nicassy. I didn't pay your lil temper tantrum an ounce of attention. Whatever qualm you have with me, is on you. If nobody knows about me, you should. So, you already know I've chalked that shit up and let you carry the burden. On my end, me and you are good. It's up to you to fix your end."

Kenzie didn't lie about anything she said and I didn't have a comeback for her. We'd been through hell and back and I let stupid shit come between what we had with one another. Deep down, I knew she was hurt by my actions, but Kenzie was the type to hide her true feelings in order to keep her hardened side in the open.

"Are you still there?" Kenzie asked.

"Yeah, I'm here. I'll be in Atlanta later today and I want us to sit down and have a conversation. Will that be possible?"

"Of course. I want you to leave all the bullshit wherever you are though. I would hate to have to beat yo' ass. I'm telling you now, we good. If you still have beef with me, air that shit out while you got me on the line. Once we hang up, the shit is dead to me, but I won't ever forget how you came at me though. Shit is not ever going to be the way it was before you got that stick stuck up your ass."

"There's no beef. I'm sorry, Kenzie. I want to work on our friendship, I really do. Look, I have to pack, so I won't keep you any longer. I'll shoot you a text when I touch down and then we can meet up. I love you, Kenzie."

Instead of responding, Kenzie hung up. It was going to take more than words to get her to forgive me and I didn't have anyone to blame but myself. We were kids when their grandma took me in after my mother died, and we had been like sisters ever since, until we started working for Heat. Shaking the memories from my head, I went to my Apple music app and went to my Chris Brown playlist. "Say Goodbye" started playing and my mind went directly to Stone.

Throwing items onto the bed as the music blared through the surround sound, I followed Stone's instructions and left behind everything he had purchased. As I slipped on a pair of leggings, I heard a noise from downstairs. Easing toward the door, the music was still playing as I crept to the stairwell to see who was in the house.

The front door was closing as I peeked over the banister but I didn't get the chance to see who had left. Racing to the window in the bedroom, Stone's car appeared on our street as he waited for a car to pass so he could turn into the driveway. My heart started beating faster because he couldn't have left the house a few moments prior. Whoever it was had dipped off quickly, because there was no one walking on the street. I walked briskly out of the bedroom and made my way to the stairs. The door opened and there was a loud explosion and the ceiling came tumbling down on top of me.

My life flashed before my eyes before I saw my mother walking toward me. I hadn't seen her beautiful face in many years and she looked good. Mama glided toward me slowly with her arms outstretched and she had the prettiest smile on her face. I knew at that moment she and I would live an eternal life together forever.

Chapter 2

Heat

Sitting in my office chair as I stared out the window, thoughts of the way I treated Summer came full force. Baby girl didn't deserve that shit, but she was in the line of fire to get the back-lash intended for Kenzie. I cared for Summer, but I knew the only thing I would do was hurt her repeatedly and I didn't want to do that to her. Hell, I knew deep down I loved Kenzie, but didn't want to be exclusive with her either. A relationship was something I just wasn't willing to put myself in when I knew for a fact, I couldn't give it my all.

When Kenzie and I were together, I treated her like she was my woman. I never told her how I felt about being tied down with just one woman. We just went with the flow and I did everything needed to keep her happy. Being that she was young, I knew all I had to do was wine and dine her, and she would be mine for the taking.

The moment Summer threw herself at me, it was on from there. Kenzie would travel for jobs and I would be in Atlanta fuckin' the shit out of Summer. One day, Kenzie came back early and caught Summer with my dick in her mouth. Usually, I would lock the door to my office, but that particular day the only thing on my mind was pussy.

Kenzie went on a rampage and Storm emerged without warning. She beat the fuck out of Summer. I tried to pull them apart and Kenzie punched my ass dead in the eye. Had a nigga seeing all kinds of stars. She stormed out of my office and never looked back. When I found out she and her sister lost their grandma and went back to Chicago, I gave her time to calm down.

I called to check on her and the conversations got shorter every time I reached out. Kenzie finally told me there was no chance of us being together because she would have to kill me. She stated if she couldn't be the only woman in my life, don't waste her time. I couldn't even think of a comeback to win her over from that shit. No woman had ever put their foot down when it came to fuckin' with me and it threw me for a loop.

From that day forward, I never had the opportunity to have a decent conversation with Kenzie. The only thing I got was hostility from Storm. I'd seen her boss up on plenty of people, but never with me. But that was all I'd been dealing with since she stepped back on the scene. She wanted to play hard ball, well I was with the shits and I hoped she was ready.

Summer was gone the morning after our disagreement, when I woke up to check on her. She must've left soon as the sun peered through the blinds. The only indication I'd received to let me know she was good was a text she'd sent to my phone. She also asked to take time off from the club, leaving me to step up and order the necessary materials she usually took care of. Business went on as usual, but the vibe in the club amongst the other employees were off.

Things had been kind of fucked up with the squad as well and I didn't expect nothing less from them young muthafuckas. The twins had Khaos and Phantom's noses wide open and it had a nigga hot under the collar. Kenzie was playing a dangerous game and didn't even know. She was going to learn the hard way not to play with me. If she couldn't stand the Heat, she should've stayed her ass out the kitchen.

I was waiting on a call from Rocko at any moment. Soon as the thought entered my mind, my phone started vibrating. Rocko's name appeared on the screen and I smiled as I picked the phone up and placed it to my ear.

"Tell me something good, nigga."

"It's done," Rocko said. "Heat, that shit was like a scene from the movie *Die Hard with a Vengeance*. There was no way anybody survived that explosion. The structure was blown to smithereens."

"'Nough said, man. You will get the entire payment for a job well done," I said, putting the phone on speaker and transferring five hundred thousand to his account. "I'll holla at you soon and we'll be back on track very soon. Don't say shit to nobody. If any questions come your way, keep yo' muthafuckin' mouth shut. Send that shit to me and I'll deal with it. We will have a meeting in a matter of days, so keep yo' line open."

"Aight, bet," Rocko said, ending the call.

One of my problems was dealt with and that shit made a nigga happy as hell. I could set the next stage of my plan in motion. With Stone out of the way, it meant more money coming straight to me. It was time to rise to the occasion and make shit shake for my team. Cutting his ass out was the best thing I could've ever done. Hell, my team was doing all the work and he benefited from it, and the only thing he'd done was provided the contracts.

I knew his clientele damn near better than he did. Once word was out that Stone was dead, they would come right where they belonged, with me. One would wonder if I felt bad about what I did. The answer would be, hell nawl! I didn't know that muthafucka personally, that shit was business and I no longer needed him. Was I greedy? Yep, and I was still hungry and would continue to eat because I was still breathing. I couldn't say the same about Stone though.

Laughing to myself, I poured a shot of Hennessy and threw it back. Now, I had to figure out a way to get Kenzie's ass back into my bed. Her ass was playing hard to get because of that nigga Phantom, but there wasn't shit his lil ass could do for her. She went from a boss to one of his workers. She would be back soon as news traveled that she'd lost someone dear to her. Stupid ass bitch.

Chapter 3

Phantom

"Daddy, wake up." Layla pounced on top of my bed, jumping around like she'd lost her damn mind. "I let you sleep long enough, now get up and fix me something to eat."

The last couple of weeks had been very trying. Layla and I had been hanging tough since Heat hadn't called about work. I was tired as hell and didn't fall asleep until well after four in the morning because I couldn't get Kenzie off my mind. I tried calling after she left my house and she didn't answer. I wasn't going to sweat her ass, she could have that shit. The pussy was good, but not good enough for me to hound her ass.

"Layla!" I said, throwing a pillow at her head. "What time is it, you brat?"

"It's time for you to wake up and feed me! I'm hungry, man."

Sitting up slightly with my hand propped on the side of my head. This child of mine had to be out of her ever-loving mind, talking to me like that. She knew better than that when it came to me.

"Who you talking to, Lay?" I asked to see how far she would go with her sassiness.

"Youuuuuuu," she said, rolling her neck.

"I don't know how you talk to other people, but you will not talk to me that way. Yes, you may be hungry, but take the attitude out of your voice before we have major problems." Layla poked her bottom lip out and tears welled in her eyes. "You bet not drop a tear," I said sternly.

Wiping at her eyes, my daughter sniffled loudly as if that shit was going to move me. I took the time she was gathering herself to swing my legs over the side of the bed and headed to the bathroom. Her lil ass needed time alone before I yanked her up by the neck. I blame her mama, because instead of teaching Layla right from wrong, Tiff was teaching her how to be the baddest bitch. Not on my watch. My daughter was going to learn to respect herself in every way possible.

As I stood at the sink brushing my teeth, Layla appeared in the doorway. "What is it, Layla?"

"Daddy, I'm sorry. Mommy lets me talk that way to her." Layla knew she fucked up. Spitting the toothpaste in the sink, I rinsed my mouth before I even attempted to chastise my one and only child.

"What happens at your mama's house isn't allowed here. As a matter of fact, I don't want to hear about you talking to yo' mama in that manner either. That's disrespectful to any adult and I want you to correct it yourself. If I have to get on you about the way you talk again, we will have serious problems, Layla. Do you understand me?"

"Yes, Daddy." She sniffled. "My mistakes help me learn and grow," Layla mumbled loud enough for me to hear.

"That's right! What else?" I asked, staring at her through the mirror.

"I am open and ready to learn."

"Damn right. Now, come on so we can get you something to eat. What do you want?" I asked, grabbing her by the hand.

The two of us walked to the kitchen and I pulled a chair out for my princess. Pushing her up to the table, I walked deeper into the kitchen as I waited for Layla to tell me what she wanted for breakfast. Tired as hell, all I wanted to do was go back to bed, but I couldn't. Duty called.

"Can I have pancakes, sausage, and eggs?"

"I got you, but you're going to help. Get the eggs, milk and cheese out the fridge. Mix them in this bowl like I taught you," I said, placing the bowl on the table along with a whisk. As I pulled my cast iron skillet from the bottom cabinet, my cell-phone rang from the living room. "Lay, run and get my phone, please."

Measuring out the pancake mix, I poured it in a bowl along with eggs and milk. Mixing all the ingredients together, I had to stop for a moment because I could've sworn I heard Layla's voice as she came down the hall. *How did go get my phone, turn into answering my phone?* Waiting for her to enter the kitchen, I leaned against the counter with a stern expression on my face.

"Mommy, I don't want to come home if Butch is going to be there." I overheard my daughter say as she tried to talk low as possible. "My daddy is not trying to keep me away from you, I don't want to come. Butch is mean, Mommy. He always hits you—" Tiff must've cut her off because she stopped talking abruptly. "Daddy is in the kitchen and can't hear me. It's true, Mommy, he's always hurting you."

I'd heard enough. Pushing off the counter, I walked out of the kitchen to find Layla sitting on the floor with my phone to her ear. Raising her eyes up at me, her little head dropped as I held my hand out for the phone. Layla was kind of hesitant about giving me the phone, but she stood to her full height of four feet five inches and passed the phone over to me.

"You need to stop talking about what goes on in my house. Butch ain't here, so why the hell won't you tell your daddy to bring you home?" Tiff thought she was still talking to my daughter and I was mad because she was basically telling Layla to keep secrets from me. "Layla, do you hear me talking to you? Tell Xavier to bring you home!"

"How dare you tell her not to tell me anything! Are you out of your mind?" I asked, walking into the spare bedroom and slamming the door. "Long as that nigga's in yo' shit, my daughter won't be. He can beat yo' ass to death without her being there to witness the shit, Tiff."

"Phan—Phantom, I didn't mean it the way you took it. Butch ain't even here, because you shot him and he moved out."

"Why tell her in not so many words to be quiet about what goes on in your house? You know what, it don't even matter. Layla won't sleep one night in that house, until I'm convinced you're done with that bum ass muthafucka!"

"You jealous, Phantom? I guess you ready to be back in my life, huh? Layla needs a mother and a father in her life." Her ghetto ass thought that bullshit was funny and really thought I gave a fuck about who she decided to lay up with. The only thing I cared about was my daughter. Her stupid ass mama could chew on glass for all I cared.

"Tiff, you and I both know that shit will never happen. If us getting back together is part of your plan, start over, sweetheart. That train ran off the tracks a long time ago. For the record, Layla has a father in her life. Her mother is the one that needs to work on getting herself together so she can be there too. I'm not about to go back and forth with you, okay? I can bring her over for a couple hours, but that's it. Don't play with me, Tiff. Run off with my daughter and I will kill yo' ass when I find you," I gritted into the phone.

"You always throwing threats, Phantom. I'm not scared of you!" she screamed.

"I don't want you to be scared, Tiff. What I do want is for you to be aware of the nigga I am. I'll call you when we're on our way."

"Don't bring yo' bitch with you either! I owe that hoe an ass whoopin' for the shit she pulled a few weeks ago." Tiff was trying to sound tough when I knew for a fact she wasn't about that life. "What the fuck's so funny?" she asked as I laughed softly.

"Nothing, man. You worry about the wrong shit. But here's a little advice for you, don't run up on that woman if you see her in the streets. It won't end well for you, Tiff. She's nothing like the other females you fought in the past, trust me."

"So, you're not going to deny she's your bitch?"

"Again, you're worrying about my life when you a bitch to a nigga that whoops yo' ass. Concentrate on getting out of that situation. What's going on with me, shouldn't be your concern. Like I said, I'll call you when we're on our way."

Hanging up on Tiff, I rubbed my hand down my face and walked out of the room. Layla was stirring the eggs and I proceeded to make the pancakes. It took about thirty minutes to finish and we sat down to eat.

"Daddy, I heard you tell Mommy we were coming over," Layla said breaking the silence with a mouthful of food. "Are you going to stay with me?"

"Nah, I'm going to allow you to spend a little time with your mama. When you're ready to leave, call me and I'll come pick you up." Layla ate her food quietly and I could sense she didn't really want to go. "If you don't want to go, all you have to do is tell me, baby girl."

"No, I'll go as long as you come back to get me."

Nodding my head, I finished my food and stood to start cleaning the kitchen while Layla finished her breakfast. After bringing her plate to me, she left to get ready for her visit to Tiffany's, but she moved hesitantly toward the stairs. I'd have to see how the visit goes in order to determine how I would proceed with Layla's visitations. Talking to my lawyer was a must, because I knew for a fact, my baby would be with me on a permanent basis.

About two hours later, we were ready to hit the road. The ponytail I pulled her hair into was neat, but could've been better. I wasn't going to worry about it though, Tiff could comb it when we got to her house. Layla settled in the backseat looking sad as she buckled her seatbelt. I stared at her through the windshield for a moment before opening the door to slide into the driver's seat.

"Lay, if you don't want to go, tell me now. We can find something else to do."

"I'm fine, Daddy. I'll go for a couple hours."

Starting the car, Lizzo's "Good as Hell" came on the radio, and I knew my baby was about to turn up. That was the only time I would even remotely allow myself to jam to a feminine ass song. I'd do anything for my princess and that was one of the times I let loose and joined in with her.

I do my hair toss
Check my nails
Baby how you feelin'?
Feelin' good as hell

I backed out the driveway slowly and pressed the brake. "Come up here with me, Lay. We're about to sing this song with our chest!"

It didn't take long for her to climb between the seats and get buckled in the front. It was rare for me to allow her to sit in the passenger seat, but I wanted to get her mind off of going to Tiffany's funky ass house. Layla reached over to start the song over and we rocked out, but it didn't stop there. We listened to any song she wanted until we pulled up to her mother's townhome.

I forgot to call Tiff to tell her we were on our way, but it shouldn't have mattered, we were there already. Layla opened the door to step out and I did the same. When I walked around the front of my car, the front door of Tiff's house opened and that nigga Butch walked out on the porch on crutches. I instantly got pissed because the bitch lied through her muthafuckin' teeth when she called earlier.

"Go back to the car, Layla," I said, without taking my eyes off the nigga.

Layla did as she was told and I stalked toward the house as Tiff stepped out. Her eyes bulged when she saw me and all I saw was red. It was the perfect opportunity for that nigga to get at me because I wasn't strapped. Butch propped himself against the railing and grilled me as I got closer.

"Nigga, let Layla out of the car! That's the reason you over here, right?" Butch addressed me.

"It's not yo' business why *I'm* here. Why the fuck is you in this muthafucka?" I shot back. "Tiff, you've lied for the last time. When you clear out yo' crib, that's when you will see my daughter. Until then, fuck you!"

"Phantom, Butch was just over here—"

"You bet not explain shit to this nigga! I'm yo' muthafuckin' man, Tiff!" Butch growled at her. The way she flinched was pitiful. His ass was on crutches and still scared the shit out of her weak ass.

Not wasting any more time going back and forth, I walked back to my whip and got in the car. Tiff came running down the stairs full speed. I put the car in drive and backed up to pull off.

"Layla, get out the car! This is my time with you," Tiff screamed. Layla glanced over at me, never looking her mother's way. "Get out!"

"She's not getting out of shit, Tiff! Move yo' ass back before I run you the fuck over." I meant every word I said and she knew it. "I already told you the stipulations on visits with my daughter. My lawyer will be contacting you soon. Get rid of that toxic nigga, if you want any type of relationship with my daughter."

I drove off without another word, trying to calm myself down. The inside of the car was silent as hell and Layla was still staring at me. Making sure to keep my eyes on the road, I glanced over at her briefly and at further glance, it appeared as if my baby was staring through me.

"Lay, what's on your mind?" I asked.

She blinked a couple times before sitting back against the seat. "Why did she lie about Butch? I don't like that man, Daddy. He is so mean."

"Layla, I'm going to ask this question and I want you to answer truthfully. Has Butch ever touched you in an inappropriate way? Any part of your body?" I asked seriously.

"No, Daddy. He only hits my mommy and I don't like that. What if he hits me next?" she asked, choking up.

"Then he will die. You are the one person, other than my mama, that I don't play about. You don't have to worry about him putting his hands on you, Layla. You live with me now," I said, reaching over to grab her hand. "Now, what do you want to do?"

"I wanna see Kenzie. Is she your girlfriend, Daddy?"

I was shocked Layla chose to be around Kenzie. They'd only met once and Layla had been asking about her ever since. I couldn't answer anything because Kenzie had been missing in action, since we had sex after returning from Minnesota. Hell, I wanted to see her sexy ass too.

"Nope, she's not my girlfriend but she is a good friend of mine." Grabbing my phone, I scrolled my contacts until I got to Kenzie's name and pressed the button to give her a call. The phone was connected to the Bluetooth and the ringing of the phone filled the car. For a minute I thought she wasn't going to answer like the other times I'd called.

"Hello, Phantom," Kenzie's sultry voice came out of the speaker's crystal clear.

"Hi, Kenzie. It's Layla."

"Layla! What a surprise. How are you?"

"I'm fine. I was telling Daddy I wanted to come over to see you. Would it be alright?" Layla asked, biting her bottom lip. The line went quiet and I thought she was going to say no and break my baby's heart.

"I'm not home, but tell your daddy to bring you to the Chipotle by my house. Do you want anything?"

"Yes, can you order me a burrito bowl with extra steak and chicken? Oh, no beans please, and lettuce, tomato, and sour cream. Extra sour cream, please."

"You got it. I'll see you when you get here, sweetheart."

Kenzie ended the call and I was stuck because she kept the conversation solely on Layla like I was a little nigga or some shit. My daughter's demeanor went from somber to one of excitement and it was all because of Kenzie. Her ass was going to have to put that hard shit in her back pocket because I was coming for her ass, whether she wanted me to or not. That silent treatment shit was for those lame niggas, not me. Accelerating just enough so I wouldn't get pulled over, I couldn't wait to be in Kenzie's presence and see her beautiful face.

Meesha

Chapter 4

MaKenzie

The last person I expected to hear from was Princess Layla. Even though I knew Phantom was behind the call, I couldn't turn down the chance for her to spend time with me. I had been dodging all of Phantom's calls since the night we had relations, because the way he pleased my body wasn't supposed to happen. I was all for fuckin', but Phantom took it to the level of lovemaking and my feelings were trying to go in a whole other direction. So, I put space between us.

Ordering Layla's and my food, I turned to walk away to find a table for us. After placing the food down, I decided to order something for Phantom since he would be there with his daughter. When his food was ready, I was heading back to the table when the door to the restaurant opened and the two of them walked in. Layla was looking cute in a jean skirt with a rainbow-colored shirt, matching tennis shoes and a little purse of the same color.

Phantom and Layla walked in my direction and she had the biggest smile on her face. I was surprised by the way she had taken to me after just one visit. It was sure to have something to do with her trifling ass mama. To be honest, I was too young to play mama to anyone's child, but that didn't mean I couldn't be a mentor in Layla's life.

"Hey, Kenzie!" Layla said happily as she rushed ahead of her daddy to hug me.

"Hey, beautiful. Look at you, looking all cute and stuff. I love that skirt!" I really did love the skirt and would rock it myself. Layla had good taste in clothes for a seven-year-old.

"Thank you! I picked it out myself when Daddy took me shopping," Layla beamed.

"You did a great job. Sit down so your food doesn't get cold," I said, helping her into the chair next to me.

I could feel Phantom's eyes burning a hole in the side of my face, but I didn't address him until I had Layla settled with her food. Sitting down in my chair, I finally laid eyes on Phantom and damned near choked on my spit. He wore a gray tank that showed off all of his tattoos, and a pair of sweat shorts that displayed the log in his pants. Closing my eyes for a spell was a mistake because the scene inside his bedroom replayed behind my eyelids.

"What's up, Storm?" he asked, taking a seat across from me.

I didn't answer right away because my throat was dry as fuck. Gulping down the water I had brought along with me, I finished the entire bottle without taking a breath. I ran my hand over my mouth and looked up at Phantom's fine ass. I chuckled lowly at the thought of him calling me by my alias.

"Oh, I'm back to being Storm, huh? Kenzie is too formal for you, Xavier?"

"Don't call me by my gov'ment, man. Look, I just came by because Layla wanted to see you. I was respecting your space. We can discuss this at another time, not now," he said nodding toward Layla.

I understood what he was saying and let it go. I pushed his food in front of him and removed the lid from mine. We were all eating quietly until Layla broke the ice.

"Kenzie, would you do my hair like yours? It's so pretty." My hair was flowing down my back and the style wasn't appropriate for a girl her age.

"Maybe when you're older, but I can give you a style with a lot of curly ponytails. That's if it's okay with your dad," I responded.

"Daddy, you wouldn't mind if Kenzie did my hair, right?"

"No, I wouldn't mind at all. Anything would be better than what I've done to your hair," Phantom replied. When would you have time to do it, Kenzie?"

"I can do it today if you want. I don't have anything to do after I leave here."

"My house or yours?" he smirked. I was definitely not going to his home. I was fighting off the flashbacks from the last time I was in the comfort of his bedroom as is.

"Since we are closer to my house, we can go there," I said, clearing my throat. "What have the two of you been up to today?"

"I went to see my mommy, but it didn't work out too good, so I asked Daddy if could come see you," Layla said as she shoved rice in her mouth. "Daddy, would you get me something to drink please? A Sprite."

"Yeah," Phantom said, standing to his feet. "Would you like something too, Kenzie?"

Digging in my purse, I removed a couple dollars and held them out to Phantom. "Get me a green tea with honey."

Phantom nodded his head and walked away without taking my money. I stared after him and squeezed my legs together because my yoni was going crazy under my jean shorts. The sight of his tattooed back turned me all the way on.

"Don't get mad at Daddy for not taking your money. He never allows a lady to pay for anything in his presence. Let him court you and treat you like a queen. He really likes you, Kenzie."

Phantom was raising his daughter to accept nothing but the best from a man. I could tell she was soaking in everything he had taught her and she was trying to pass it on to me. I nodded my head in agreement as I continued eating.

"What makes you think he likes me?" I asked.

"He never brings me around a woman that's not my mama. My daddy doesn't let anyone other than family to get close. That says a lot to me. Do you like my daddy?"

Opening my mouth to respond, I snapped it shut because Phantom was coming back toward the table. He sat down and I thanked him for the beverage and continued eating my food. I really wanted to be out of his sight since Layla spilled the tea on his ass. I liked him too, but I wasn't trying to be his woman.

"So, what have you been up to, Kenzie?" Phantom asked.

"Nothing much. I've just been waiting around for Heat to hit us with a job. He's been on some fuck shit." My head snapped in Layla's direction. "I'm sorry for my language, Layla."

"It's okay. I hear that type of talk all the time," she said, hunching her shoulders as she continued to eat.

"Just because you hear it, doesn't make it right. I'm gon' break you out of that mindset, Layla. It seems you're itching to find out what punishment is like. Believe me, you won't like it," Phantom said sternly. "I want you to stay a kid as long as possible, enjoy this stage of your life. You have never been on the receiving end of my rants, keep it that way."

Phantom's jaw was flexing rapidly as he stared at his daughter. I understood where he was coming from with what he said to Layla, but it wasn't my business to intervene. I didn't know nothing about being a parent. That was my cue to get us out of the establishment before he had her crying in public.

"We should head over to my place so Miss Layla can get her hair done. Maybe we can go to Dave & Buster's or something so she can have some fun," I suggested as Phantom's jaw relaxed as I stared at him. "What do you think, Dad?"

He didn't respond right away because he had started eating again. Layla looked like she was praying to the entertainment gods that he would say yes to going out to have fun. Phantom glanced across the table at his daughter and nodded his head slowly as he swallowed the last of the food he chewed into mush. I helped Layla close up what was left of her food and stood to get a few bags from the cashier. None of us finished our lunch, but Chipotle was always good the second time around, so there wasn't going to be a waste.

After packing everything up, my mind focused on how I was going to bring a smile to Layla's little face. She gravitated to me in such a short time and I was going to be a part of her life, even though I wasn't trying to be too close with Phantom. A girl needed a woman to teach her how to carry herself in the proper manner.

Layla rushed around the table, grabbing hold of my hand while clutching the bag that held her food. Looking down at her, I smiled because she was a female version of her daddy. Her trifling ass mama had nothing to do with her appearance into the world, other than pushing her out. As we walked to the exit, Layla stopped in her tracks and glanced back at the table.

"Daddy, I left my purse on the table." Layla let my hand go and walked back to retrieve her purse.

"I'll meet y'all outside. I'm going to my car so I can turn the air on. It's hot as hell out there," I said, glancing up at Phantom. He nodded his head as he gripped his bottom lip into his mouth as he stared at me.

"Don't think I haven't noticed you've been avoiding me, Kenzie. We'll talk about that shit real soon. I'm gon' let you think you're pulling one over on me. But it won't be too much longer."

I rolled my eyes and walked out the door without responding to him. My yoni was cussing me out because she wanted his python to caress her folds, but the bitch was not about to speak for me that day. Hurrying to get away from Phantom, I made my exit as I dug around in my purse for my keys. Lifting my head, I noticed a silver Monte Carlo creeping up the street.

Not thinking anything of it, I continued on to my car without any worries. Tires burning against the pavement caught my attention and my eyes zoomed in on the car. The passenger window lowered and I knew something was about to go down. An arm extended outward and there was a bitch behind the gun she held, but I didn't get to see her face because she started bustin' at my ass.

My reflexes were on point and I dove to the ground and rolled under the car next to mine to dodge the bullets. When the gunfire ceased, I crawled from my position but the car was bending the corner out of sight. Phantom was jogging down the street as I stood to my feet.

"Where is Layla?" I asked, looking around frantically.

"I made her stay inside when I heard the shots. I tried to get at 'em, but they peeled out. You good?" he asked, looking me over to make sure I wasn't hit.

"I'm alright. Who the fuck was that? And why they gunnin' for me?"

Phantom had fire in his eyes and I could tell he knew exactly who tried to take me out. "I didn't get to see who was inside the whip, but whoever it was didn't hit their target and will try that shit again. The reason is unknown until we find out who it was."

"I'll be ready because I'm not beefing with no muthafuckin' body. If I find out who took a shot at me, it's over for them, Phantom." I was heated and couldn't stop myself from looking around frantically. To be honest, I was hoping the coward ass muthafuckas bent the corner and came back.

"You promised Layla a day out and we're going to take her to have fun. One thing I don't do is disappoint my daughter. Save that shit for another day. Get out of Storm mode for

Layla, okay?" Phantom was practically begging me to let the shit go. I didn't agree but I had to because he was right, I did hype Layla up for our outing.

"You got it. My kill radar is on an all-time high," I said, grabbing my purse from the ground before jumping in my ride.

Phantom went inside to get Layla and I waited until they were situated in his car before I backed out of the parking spot heading home.

Meesha

Chapter 5

Loco

"How the fuck did you miss, Mya? The bitch was standing right there and you had a clear shot!"

"Loco, why didn't you shoot her yourself, tough guy? Stop screaming at me before we end up fighting in this mutha-fuckin' car. Hurry up and get back to the house."

Mya was on the verge of getting knocked the fuck out. She had one job and couldn't even follow through with the task. Storm and Kane was going to wish they never came back to Atlanta once I was finished with them. Hopefully, after the near-death experience, whichever one almost got hit, would run scared. Those two bitches were taking my shine.

"Why did you want me to shoot at that girl anyway? Is she threatening to expose you for cheating again, Loco?"

"Ain't nobody cheating on yo' funky ass!" I snapped. "That bitch, or her sister, pistol whipped me a few weeks ago."

"Now the truth comes out," she laughed. "You must not remember telling me you got jumped by a bunch of niggas. Why lie to me, of all people, about what happened? I wouldn't have judged you. If anything, I could've beat the fuck outta the bitches before now."

"Mya, these bitches are like straight up niggas. You—"

"Loco, where can I find them? All that other shit is irrelevant. I can go toe to toe with yo' ass, so a couple of females ain't shit to me."

"I think one of them is fuckin' with Phantom," I said, taking my eyes off the road for a second.

"Phantom! I wonder if Tiff knows about his ass messing with some bitch."

Mya was the messiest female around. She knew damn well Tiffany and Phantom been done. The only thing they had between the two of them was Layla. If she was going to bring Tiff in to handle the twins, they better whoop ass, because it would be their only chance.

"Tiff has a whole man out there, Mya. She can't even trip on Phantom. Whatever you do, don't tell her about what happened today. That stays between me and you. We will for sure have a target on our backs if word got out that I was involved in that drive-by."

"The way you said that has me thinking you're scared, Loco. Where's the hardcore nigga I fell in love with? You're sounding like a whole female in this muthafucka." Mya laughed like a hyena and I didn't appreciate it one bit.

WHAP! I slapped the taste outta her mouth and drew blood. Her eyes bucked with shock as I pulled into our driveway. Mya wiped her mouth with the back of her hand and glared at me as if she was going to swing back. Instead, she opened the door and got out of my whip. I watched as she walked up the steps and entered our home.

I used to whoop her ass faithfully when we first got together, but after she started going on jobs with me, all that shit went out the window. But there were times when her mouth got her in trouble and I would pop her ass. In return, we would have a downright brawl then fuck afterwards. Yeah, our relationship was toxic as fuck and it's been working for us for years. There's no need to switch things up.

I exited the car, making my way into the house and shut the door behind me, Mya came out of nowhere and hit me with a two-piece combo and kicked me in my stomach. Doubling over, I held my shit, cussing under my breath.

"What I tell you about your hands, Loco? You ain't Ike, and I'm not about to be your Tina! We can kill each other in this muthafucka before I let you just beat my ass!"

Mya stood with her chest heaving up and down. She looked like an angry bull ready to attack, but I couldn't let her get away with punching my ass like she did. I stood up and towered over her small frame before grabbing her by the throat and lifted her off the floor.

"Watch yo' fuckin' mouth and we wouldn't be going through all of this bullshyt!" I growled in her face. "Stay in a woman's place and things would be better for you. But if you raise your hand at me, this is what yo' ass gon' get," I said, headbutting her in the middle of her forehead.

Why did I do that stupid shit? My head started pounding instantly because my wounds weren't completely healed. Before I knew what was happening, Mya reached up and clawed my eyes with her nails and I dropped her without thought. Scrambling back to her feet, she grabbed a handful of my dick and squeezed with all her might. I yelped like a wounded dog and the shit paralyzed me until she released me. My breath was caught in my throat because my dick was throbbing.

"Think about what you did and don't let it happen again. It's over, so don't come for me again, because I won't have a problem shooting you in your fuckin' pinky toe."

My phone started ringing and I glared at Mya but left her alone for the moment. As I pulled my phone from my pocket, she eased her little ass out of the room. Pushing the talk button on my phone, I put the phone to my ear.

"What up?" I asked, sitting on the couch, rubbing my junk.

"Loco, how's things going, fam?" Rocko asked on the other end of my line.

"Shit my head is hurting like a muthafucka, but I'm good. Everything's straight with you? Shid, you don't call me out the blue like this."

Rocko was quiet for a few seconds, then took a deep breath. "Yeah, I just wanted to check on you since you've been out of commission for a minute. Plus, I wanted to let you know that we'll be having a meeting soon. Be looking out for a call from Heat."

"Oh, that was a minor setback and I'm almost good as new. I appreciate you checking on me. Hopefully, we will be back to business soon. I need to get the fuck away from Mya before I beat the fuck outta her. I won't be coming to the meeting, but I'll inform Heat when he hits my line." Mya walked into the room, sitting on the loveseat across from me. Ignoring her, I tuned back in to what Rocko was saying.

"Well, rest up, my nigga. We don't need you back in the field until you're a hunnid percent. The team can hold shit down until you return. Try not to murder Mya in the process," he laughed. "Jail is the last place you want to be, Loco. Maintain your composure, fam. I'll check in with you soon."

"Aight, bet. Keep me updated about what's going on."

"Fo sho. I'm out," Rocko said, ending the call.

Mya sat with a scowl on her face and her arms folded over her chest. She looked like a spoiled ass child. Shaking my head, I placed my phone beside me. "What, Mya?" I asked irritably.

"You need a ride to the meeting?"

"There's no meeting. You listening too hard, always in my fuckin' business," I snapped.

"I'm about to go get LJ from my mama then." Mya got up and grabbed her keys. "Do you need anything before I leave?"

"Nah, I know you up to bullshit, Mya. Go get my son and bring yo' ass right back. If I have to come looking for you, we gon' have a problem." She rolled her eyes and switched out the door. Once I heard Mya pull out of the driveway, I headed to the kitchen for a bottle of water. My head was pounding and pain medicine was needed for the headache taking over my whole being. My eyes were blurred and I could hear my heartbeat in my ears.

Walking slowly up the stairs with the water bottle in hand, I stepped into my bedroom and stood inside the doorway for a spell trying to figure out where the hell I placed my medicine. When I spotted the pills on my nightstand, I rushed forward and popped two. Before I knew it, I was sprawled on top of the covers and sleep took over.

Meesha

Chapter 6

Celeste

It's been four days since Sam came ringing my doorbell like a mad woman. When she told me my brother's house was blown up, I fell to my knees and the pain in my chest was excruciating. Never in a million years did I ever think anything would happen to Stone.

Sam and I raced into the hospital and I fell into my father's arms soon as I spotted him and my mama in the waiting room. We were told Stone was in a coma from being hit with debris from the explosion. I'd been trying to figure out how the house blew up for days, but nothing came to mind.

I've sat by Stone's bedside every day thereafter and he hadn't stirred once. The doctors kept telling us his vitals were very good but they couldn't explain why he wasn't waking up. The hardest part of it all was explaining to my brother that Angel died that day. I still couldn't believe she was gone. In my opinion, she was the best woman for Stone and I knew her death was going to destroy him.

"Come on, bro. You gotta wake up," I said, caressing the back of Stone's hand. The doctor told us to talk to him because he would be able to hear us and it could help him come out of the coma. "You're going to come out of this stronger than you were before all this shit happened. I need you, Savon."

A lone tear fell from my eye, seeing my brother lying lifeless in the hospital bed. The only indication that he was alive was the heart monitor that beeped steadily on the other side of his bed. I'd always told him to take a break from working so much. I didn't mean for it to be forced upon him though. My mind went back to when we were younger and the thought brought a smile to my face.

"Remember when Daddy bought me a new bike and I didn't want the training wheels on it? You spent days trying to teach me how to ride," I paused, intertwining his hand with mine. "Every time I fell and scraped a part of my body, you kissed it and told me to get my ass up and try again. I wanted to punch the shit out of you. But you never gave up on me. It's my turn to push you, Savon. I won't allow you to give up. You have to fight."

The sound of a phone ringing interrupted my conversation with my brother. I reached into my purse and pulled out my phone but it wasn't mine. I trained my ears on the sound and opened the drawer of the nightstand. Stone's phone was connected to the charger and Sam must've been the one that placed it there. Quickly pressing the green icon, I put the phone to my ear.

"Hello," I said lowly.

"Yeah, let me speak to Stone," the caller replied.

Rising to my feet, I looked at my brother before I made my way to the door. I stepped out the room and closed the door behind me. "Who is this?" I asked curiously. At that point, I didn't trust a soul because nobody knew why this happened to my brother and Angel.

"My name is Scony. I was looking for Stone, maybe I dialed the wrong number. My bad, ma."

"No, you have the right number. How do you know my brother?" I wanted to know everything about this muthafucka.

"We do business together. If it makes you feel any better, we own Club Onyx together. You interrogating a nigga so I want you to know that me and Stone fucks with each other." I didn't say anything in response to what he said. I was still skeptical because I'd never heard of this man a day in my life. "Look, I just need to ask him if he'd heard anything from my sis, Angel."

Hearing him say Angel's name, I sat in the nearest chair and my heart started beating fast. Angel's family didn't know what happened to her and I was the one that would have to break the news to her brother. I swallowed hard and took a deep breath before addressing the man on the other end of the phone.

"Scony, is it?" I asked, trying to stall a little bit.

"Yeah. My name is Scony. Where's Stone, shawty?" The tone of his voice was sharp, an indication that he was getting pretty irritated with me.

"Stone has been in the hospital for the past four days. He's in a coma, Scony. His house blew up and we don't know what caused the explosion. I'm sorry if I—"

"What the fuck you mean his house blew up? Where's my sister? Did she get on the plane to Atlanta?" he shouted.

The thought racing through my mind was, *why would she be on a plane to Atlanta?* She hadn't said anything about leaving Houston. I was sure she would've called and told me if she needed to leave in a hurry. Clearing my throat, I closed my eyes to deliver the devastating news to Angel's brother. I didn't know how to even begin to tell him Angel was dead. There was no other way around it except to hit him with the news.

"No. Angel didn't get on the plane. She was in the house when it exploded. I'm sorry to be the one to tell you this, but Angel didn't make it. She died four days ago," I sobbed.

The sound of that grown man crying broke me down. The hurt could be felt through the airwaves and I knew how he was feeling, because I felt the same way when I found out what happened. No words came to my mind to even attempt to console him. It didn't matter because after a few minutes, the line went dead. Contemplating calling back, I decided to give him time to process what I revealed before trying to reach out to him again.

I was shaking because I really wanted to call Scony back. Instead, I walked back into my brother's room and nothing had changed. He was still lying still with his chest rising and falling at a normal pace. Taking a seat in the chair, I once again took my brother's hand and just held it. The warmth of his touch calmed me and I began to relax. Moving the chair closer to his bed, I laid my head on the pillow and prayed for my brother to come out of the coma.

"Lord, please place your hands upon Savon and bring him back to us. He didn't deserve this, Lord. I know not to question your work, but you have to heal my brother and allow him to walk out of this hospital. I look to you to make this right. In Jesus' name, Amen."

At that moment, my phone rang and I dug inside my purse to retrieve it. Without releasing my brother's hand, I accepted the call and dreaded it the minute I answered. Joe was yelling before I could say hello.

"Where the fuck you at, Celeste?"

"Joe, I'm at the hospital. What's wrong?" I asked, putting the phone on speaker.

"Yo' ass should be at home. You've been at that damn hospital every day since yo' brother been in that muthafucka! Bring yo' ass home!"

He had to be out of his mind to call as if he was the boss of me. Joe had been calling to get my location so he could frolic around with one of his hoes without my knowledge. Acting as if he wanted me home to spend time gave his ass away because he couldn't care less and I was cool with that. When I told him about the baby, he automatically wanted me to get an abortion, until I told him it was too late.

"Of course, I have. With my brother is where I'm supposed to be. You sound stupid as hell right now, Joe."

"Where is yo' dyke ass sister? Yo' mama and daddy? Ain't none of them muthafuckas there to watch over that nigga? You don't need to be stressing about Stone's fuck-ups. I need you home with me!"

I chuckled lowly because he was putting on a theatrical performance and I knew for a fact he didn't mean none of that shit. Joe didn't give two fucks about me being at that house. The moment I stepped foot inside, he was going to talk his shit and leave soon after. Those days were over and I wasn't falling for it anymore. All he would do was threaten to leave. At this point, he can move the fuck around because he was putting too much stress on me.

"I'm not about to leave my brother's side for you or anyone else, Joe. I would never make you choose to be there for your family over me. If anything, I'd be by your side holding your hand. Where is your compassion for what's going on with my family?"

"Yo family don't like me, so why the fuck should I be there while you're watching a nigga lay in a bed? You got me fucked up, Celeste. You wasting your time just sitting and there hasn't been any change in all this time. Have you forgot you're pregnant?"

"What do me being pregnant have to do with my brother? Me being here for him is not putting me in jeopardy. As far as my family not liking you, it's because of the way you treat me, Joe. At least act like you give a fuck about me and maybe they would come around."

"They don't ever have to say anything to me! I don't have to portray myself in a way that will appease them. You are my bitch and ain't shit they can do about that. Now, for the last time, bring yo' ass home!"

"I'm staying with my brother, Joe. Stay mad because you won't prevent me from doing what I have to do for my family." I ended the call and knew once I decided to leave the hospital, Joe was going to be on bullshit. Regardless, I was ready to face him head on.

My head snapped in the direction of Stone's bed and I looked down at my hand. His fingers were wrapped around my hand in a tighter manner than when I had first grabbed it. That gave me hope and I smiled as I kissed the back of his hand. Choosing the *Victory Lap* album on my phone, I let Nipsey's voice fill the room while I closed my eyes and prayed.

Chapter 7

Scony

I had been trying to call Nicassy to see if everything was cool with her, but she wasn't responding. Stone's phone was going straight to voicemail and I was ready to take flight because I had a feeling in the pit of my stomach I couldn't shake. Sitting back for a few days, I decided to call both of their phones again. Nicassy's phone went into voicemail and I quickly called Stone. What I didn't expect was someone to answer, telling me sis was gone.

Without getting full detail of what was going on, I banged on shawty because I was wearing my feelings on my sleeve. Nicassy didn't have any family besides us and I was not ready to go to Houston to identify her body. The news I received wasn't what I expected. My heart was hurting as if I had been punched in the chest.

"Damarius, what's the matter?" Jade asked, walking into my mancave.

Shaking my head, I picked up my glass of Rémy and downed the dark liquid in one gulp. The words were twirling around in my head but they wouldn't come out of my mouth. So, I sat quietly with tears forming in my eyes. What I wasn't going to do was let this shit weaken me. Stone needed to come out of this stat, because I had questions that needed to be answered.

"Baby, answer me. What's going on?" My wife had a worried look on her face because she hadn't seen me this way since my nephew and grandma died.

"Nicassy is dead," I said, looking up at her.

"What? How? What happened?" Jade sat beside me and hugged me tightly. I shrugged her off because I didn't need to be babied at the moment.

"She called saying she was on a job, but she didn't carry through with the hit. During the conversation with her, I found out she was sent to kill my business partner. I told her to leave, but I believe she went along with her plan to tell him how she came into his life."

"You mean to tell me that nigga killed her!" Jade shrieked.

"I don't think he had anything to do with her being killed. I'm not a hunnid percent sure because he's in a coma. Hopefully, he didn't have a hand in this shit because I don't have a problem with killin' his ass. It don't matter what type of business we have together because my family comes before any other relationship. I have to call the morgue in Houston so I can properly bury Nicassy. This is fucked up."

Dropping my head in my hands, I thought about the last time I'd actually laid eyes on Nicassy. Kenzie and Kayla came to mind and I groaned loudly. "My sisters are going to have a fit. How the fuck am I supposed to tell them she's gone?"

"Just take a few minutes to gather yourself before placing that call. Maybe you should head to Houston and then pay the twins a visit before you head back home."

"Yeah, I guess it would be better for me to tell them face-to-face."

"Do you want me to go with you?" Jade asked hugging me from behind.

"Nah, stay here with Malikhi. I'll be back in a few days. You can help me pack while I make the call to get the jet ready."

Jade kissed me on the side of my mouth and walked toward the stairs. She turned to face me with worry in her eyes.

"Give G a call, Scony. I don't want you traveling alone right now. Anything can happen and your mind isn't very clear."

"I'll call him for you. The last thing I need is for you to be worrying about me. I love you, Jade."

"I love you too, baby," she said, climbing the stairs slowly.

Once I was alone, I poured another drink and downed it just as fast. Hesitating to make the call to G, the news I had for him was going to set him off. Nicassy and the twins were his sisters just as much as mine. The last conversation I had with Nicassy rang in my ears and I had a feeling that nigga Heat may have had a lot to do with what transpired.

When I landed in Atlanta, my ass was going to find out more on his ass. He better hope his fingerprints weren't left behind, because anybody associated with his ass was going to die. Listening to the phone ring as I called G, I poured more Rémy in my cup as the line connected.

"What's up, bro?"

"Man, some shit went down with Nicassy. I have to go to Houston and was wondering if you would roll with me. It's spur of the moment and I'll understand if you can't go with me."

"Nah, if you need me, I'm there. What the hell is she doing in Houston?" G asked.

"She was on a job and contacted me about the assignment. Nicassy fell for the mark and didn't complete the hit. The target was Stone, G. I advised her to pack up and leave but she was adamant about telling him the truth."

"What did that nigga do to her, Scony? It seems like you're beating around the bush. I know that's your boy and he's cool people, but that shit means nothing to me if he lost his cool with Nicassy."

I rubbed my hand down my face because G wasn't about to take this news well. The anger could be heard in his voice and I had no other choice but to tell him the truth. Throwing the shot back, I placed the glass on the table and sat back against the chair.

"G, I have to fly out to Houston to identify Nicassy's body. There was an explosion at Stone's house and she was inside. Stone is in a coma. I don't know if he's responsible for her death, but I'm not ruling him out."

"Nawl, dog. Don't tell me that. She can't be gone. Sis had so much life to live and didn't deserve that shit happening to her. What time do you want to leave?"

"I'm about to call for the jet to be ready in about an hour or so. This shit is eating at me, man, because I told her to leave the day everything happened," I said, banging my knuckles on the table.

"How did you find out about all this?"

"I was calling both Stone's and sis phone but both was going into voicemail. I finally called Stone's number and a female answered. She told me Nicassy was dead and Stone had been in a coma for the past four days. I hung up without getting any further information, but I will be calling back when I touch down in Houston."

"Aight. I'm about to pack a bag and holla at Nova. Let me know what time we heading out, and I'll be there. Did you tell Kenzie and Kayla?"

"No, when we finish up in Houston, we will head to Atlanta to see them. I don't want to tell them about this over the phone," I explained.

"Get everything together and hit my line, bro. This is fucked up. Let me get off this phone. Do what you have to do and I'll be ready to go."

I ended the call with G and made the call to my pilot. We would be set to go within the hour and I was on pins and needles about everything that had gone on. Once again, I was heading to the morgue to identify someone I loved and wasn't ready for any of it.

***

Arriving in Houston, G and I went straight to the medical examiner's office. It took several hours for us to find out if Nicassy was actually in the morgue. The body was charred and unidentifiable. The only information they could give was, the body was removed from Stone's residence.

"I would like for y'all to ship my sister's remains to Chicago. The cost doesn't matter, so just let me know the dollar amount. I can't stay in Houston to wait on the transport, but I will surely have the funeral home there to pick her up on the other end. If that's going to be a problem, let me know now."

The medical examiner stood staring with a nervous expression and he opened his mouth to speak. Before he could utter a vowel, I pulled an envelope from my back pocket that would help him make the right decision. Thumbing through the crisp, one-hundred-dollar bills, his ass slid the envelope into his lab coat and nodded his head at me.

"Don't try no slick shit because I'll hunt yo' ass down like a dog and blow yo' head clean off yo' shoulders. My sister better be delivered on time and with no delays. Are we understood?"

"Yeah, yeah. I understand. I'll make the arrangements myself and will get in touch with you when she is on her way. As a matter of fact, I will make the trip personally to be sure the delivery goes as planned," the medical examiner said, shifting from foot to foot.

"Bet. That's what I'm talking about, work for those bands."

G and I walked out of the building the same way we entered. It was a good thing we weren't able to view the body because my mind went straight to goon mode as we jumped into the rental. All that soft shit went out the window and it was time to pay Stone a visit.

Chapter 8

Stone

Hearing the loud boom when I opened the door to my house, all I remembered was getting blown back onto the ground and something hard hitting me upside the head. Struggling to open my eyes, Angel's screams filled my ears and I saw myself trying to save her. My head was banging. I ran fast as I could to get to her, but it seemed as if I was running in place. No matter how hard I fought, the scene never changed and I was going nowhere.

Everything turned black and all I could hear was a beeping noise. Out of nowhere, Celeste's voice could be heard wherever I was. She sounded like she was arguing with someone and I strained to hear what was being said. My sis was explaining that she was in the hospital. At that moment, I knew she was there with me. I'd survived but I couldn't move a muscle.

The more she talked, the clearer it became that she was talking to that bitch ass nigga, Joe. He was talking big shit because my sister was basically letting him know that she wasn't leaving my side. Joe had a lot of nerve trying to tell her to leave me alone. My bond with my sisters couldn't be broken by any muthafucka, it didn't matter who they were.

Celeste ended the call and I felt her head as she rested it on the pillow I was lying on. As I fought hard to open my eyes, my sister was praying with her whole heart for me to wake up. Little did she know, I was trying with everything within me. Celeste said amen and I could finally see the dimmed lighting in the room.

"When I see that nigga, I'm whooping his ass," I croaked. My throat was dry as hell and my voice came out like an eighty-year-old man that smoked a pack of cigarettes a day. Celeste dropped my hand and sat up quickly. She didn't respond to what I said about that nigga but her excitement made me feel good on the inside.

"Savon! Oh my God, you're awake!" she squealed, throwing her body on top of me.

"Girl, if you don't get yo' ass up," I laughed. "How long have I been in here?"

"Four days. You were hit upside the head with some debris from the house. I'm so glad you're okay. I need to call Mama and Daddy," she said, reaching for her phone.

"Nah, don't do that just yet. Celeste, where is Angel?" My sister turned her head away from me and I saw a tear glide down her face. "Sis, what's wrong?"

Celeste wiped slid her hand down her face before allowing me to look in her eyes. "Savon, Angel never made it out of the house. She died, bro."

"No, she got out. She got out! I told her to leave and she left. There's no way she was in the house when it blew up!" I screamed. "Where is Angel, sis?"

"Savon, she's dead," Celeste cried. "I'm sorry to be the one to tell you, but she's gone. Angel didn't make it out."

Bad as I wanted to cry, I couldn't. Anger took the place of the hurt and all I could think about was getting revenge. Even though the way Angel entered my life was a lie, the love she had for me was real and she showed it every day. If she truly wanted to murder me, she had plenty of chances to carry that shit out. I was going to call and tell her that I didn't care how she came into my life, she belonged by my side. But I would never get the opportunity to tell her.

The last conversation we had played in my head and I sat up straight in the bed. This shit had Heat written all over it and I was going to kill his bitch ass, soon as I got released from the fuckin' hospital. Looking around the room for my phone, Celeste followed my every move.

"Where's my phone, sis? I have to call Angel's brother. I need to tell him what happened before he comes for me."

"I already told him. His name is Scony, right?" Nodding my head slowly, I waited for her to continue with her story. "He called a few hours ago and the only thing I was able to tell him was, Angel died in an explosion. Scony hung up before I could tell him anything else. Why would he come after you, Savon? You didn't do anything."

"I know I didn't do anything, Celeste, but her brother may think differently. I called Scony to tell him about the bitch that was sent to kill me and turned out, he was her brother."

"Who was sent to kill you?" Celeste asked, interrupting me.

"Angel. Her name isn't even Angel, it's Nicassy. She was a hitwoman, sent to kill me. Instead of doing what she was sent to do, we got to know each other on another level and she aborted the mission. Celeste, I believe both of us were targeted because Angel, I mean Nicassy, went against the grain."

"Somebody is out to kill you! Why would anybody want to take you from us, Savon?" Celeste whispered in a shaky voice.

"The less you know, the better, sis. I'm gon' get to the bottom of this shit. Whoever came for me, should've made sure I was dead too. That's where they fucked up. Don't say nothing to anyone, not even Sam. Let me handle this, Celeste. Now, go out there and tell one of those nurses I'm awake and my head hurts. I need something to stop this shit."

***

Opening my eyes, my vision focused slowly. The medication the nurse administered into my IV knocked my ass out in a matter of minutes. Celeste must've gone home because she wasn't rushing to my side when I moved. As I turned my head toward the door, I noticed someone staring at me from the chair Celeste occupied earlier.

"It's about time you woke the fuck up."

"How long you been here, Scony?" I asked, trying my best to sit up.

The scowl on Scony's face let me know he wasn't there to see if a nigga was alright. There was more to his presence and it wasn't long before he got to the point. My business partner looked as if he wanted to shoot me between the eyes, but was holding back.

"It doesn't matter. What I need to know is what the fuck happened to my sister." Scony leaned forward with his elbows on his knees as he continued to stare daggers into my soul.

"I don't know. Hell, I didn't find out she was dead until earlier today. All I remember from that day is after I talked to you, I went back to the house to talk to Angel—"

"Her name was Nicassy, muthafucka!" Scony yelled as he stood.

Lying my head against the pillow, I closed my eyes because I still couldn't believe I let my guard down for a female. "Angel is what I knew her by, because that's how she introduced herself. Nicassy didn't mean shit to me until you mentioned that shit when I called you. So, as far as I'm concerned, her name is Angel," I said calmly.

"As I was saying, I went back to the house to talk to her and when I opened the front door, the house exploded. My sister informed me she died when I woke up earlier today. I'm sorry, Scony, but I didn't put a hand on her. Before I blacked out, I prayed she'd already left after I told her to leave."

"She's dead because of you, Stone!" Scony yelled, slowly walking to the bed with his fists clenched.

"Hold up, bro," a voice said from the other side of the room. My attention redirected toward the voice. G, Scony's best friend intervened, putting a hand on his chest. "I believe him. You're hurt and it's clouding yo' judgement. From what you told me, Stone is a straight-up nigga and regardless how Nicassy came into his life, he loved her. Believe me when I tell you, I wanted to come in here and blow his shit back, but he didn't do this."

I'd heard a lot about G before I met him the day me and Scony sealed the deal to open the club together. We hung out for a couple days and we all got acquainted. G would come through to check shit out at the club, but we weren't close like Scony and I was. He was basically filling in when Scony couldn't.

Scony's demeanor started to soften and he unclenched his fists. Running his right hand over his face, he shook his head ferociously as if he was trying to get something off his mind. The only thing I could do was hope he didn't attack me while I was down, because I would definitely be back in a coma.

"I hear what you saying but I need to know who the fuck could've done this shit! My family is laid up in the morgue, unrecognizable. That was a hit for yo' ass!" Scony's last words resonated in my mind and things became clear. This shit had Heat written all over it and that nigga was going to pay for it.

"I gotta get out the fuck out of here." Trying to sit up, a dizzy spell took over my body. There was no way I would be able to leave the hospital without being discharged.

"You just came out of a coma, Stone. Don't try to move ahead of yourself. Getting better should be your main priority right now." G was right, but I needed to get to Atlanta soon as possible. Heat couldn't get away with the snake shit he'd pulled. "Who did this, Stone?"

"Heat. That's the only person who could've arranged a hit for me. I don't have beef with no muthafuckin' body. When Angel told me she was hired to kill me and Heat was behind it, his ass is on top of the totem pole."

"Let Scony and I handle things until you're better. We are heading to Atlanta after leaving here. I'll keep you posted on any new information we find out. If you are connected with Nicassy's death, disappear, because you are a dead man. Mark my words."

G walked backwards and pulled Scony along with him. I understood why Scony was angry and I would've been the same way if it was one of my sisters that was killed. The difference with me, I would've killed without asking questions. It was good thing G was there to intervene because Scony wanted to dismantle my ass and I was innocent in the situation.

Buzzing for the nurse, I laid back and closed my eyes to stop the banging going on in my head. Sheila, the nurse on duty, walked in and knew exactly what I needed to help soothe the aches and pain. Soon as the meds hit my system, I started drifting off into a deep sleep with a lot on my mind.

Chapter 9

MaKenzie

Heat finally called for us to meet at the club. The shooting outside of Chipotle was still on my mind and had me moving a tad bit differently. The shit pissed me off and had me worried at the same time, because I didn't know who the fuck came for me. My Sig's been ready and off safety ready to pop off.

Rushing to finish getting dressed, my phone chirped with a text and I continued what I was doing, instead of looking to see who was on the other end. As I pulled the "Damn Right I'm Black" shirt over my head, my phone started ringing and I huffed because someone was impatient as hell on my line. Snatching my phone from the bed, I pressed the phone icon and answered aggressively.

"What?"

"Kenzie, don't get fucked up. What's your problem?"

"Phantom, what you want? I'm trying to get ready so I can get to the club."

"I wanted to know if you wanted me to come scoop you up. Since that shit happened—"

Cutting his ass right the fuck off, I snapped. "I don't need a babysitter. I'm capable of getting to my destination without an escort. Thanks, but no thanks. You don't need to come out of your way just to pick me up. Now, is there anything else I can help you with?"

"Nah, you got it, shawty. See you when I see you," he said, hanging up on my ass.

Phantom was trying hard to be the man in my life, but I knew being with him would cause more problems than good. Heat had been blowing my phone up and I hadn't answered, until he texted about work. There was nothing he and I had to conversate about if it wasn't money involved. I was good on all the "who's gonna get Kenzie" bullshit. Hell, my ass was good without a man.

After I styled Layla's hair, she's been calling me nonstop just to talk about her day. She was my lil homie and I answered each and every time. I didn't believe she really wanted to talk to me as much as she has because Phantom somehow always ended up on the other end of the line. Each time, I found a reason to get off the phone because I wasn't trying to hear shit he was talking about.

As I hopped up and down into my jeans, a slight chuckle fell from my lips because my ass was thick. Slipping my feet into my hunter green Chucks, I tied the laces and admired myself in the floor-length mirror to see how I looked. Usually, I didn't wear makeup, but I wanted to try something different for the day. Applying eyeshadows of red, green and black on my eyelids, to match the colors in my shirt, I topped my look off with nude lips. My ass was fine without trying and I was satisfied.

Collecting my keys and black Louis Vuitton wristlet, I was ready to hit the streets. Walking out of my bedroom, I doubled back to retrieve my life line. My phone. I could never leave home without it. The scene from Chipotle flashed before my eyes and I headed straight for my closet and grabbed my custom Sig with the green handle from the safe. After inspecting the clip, I stuffed the gun in the back of my jeans, snatched an extra clip and sashayed out of the door.

Backing out of my driveway, I hit the button to turn on the radio. The thought of hooking my phone to the Bluetooth didn't dawn on me, so the local station would do until I had the opportunity to safely connect my shit. Brandy's voice crooned through the speakers as she sang the chorus of "Missing You." The lyrics took me back in time and I automatically picked up my phone to call Nicassy. When I got her voicemail, it was like a dark cloud swarmed me. I couldn't place the feeling but I shook it off and continued driving.

It took twenty minutes for me to get through heavy traffic to the club. Happy hour was in full effect because the parking lot was packed. I was late as usual but I didn't give a damn. All I wanted was an assignment so I could make some money, but I had a feeling it wouldn't run that easily. Entering Heat's establishment, I walked through like I owned that muthafucka. All eyes were on me and I loved that shit.

Turning my head to the left, there were a couple bitches sitting at the bar with mean mugs on their faces, congregating with Summer's ass. One of the females stood out and I recognize her instantly. It was Phantom's baby mama and she was still mad from the paws I'd put on her ass. If they knew like I did, they would keep that shit within their circle. Laughing lowly to myself, I made my way to the conference room without a care in the world.

The door was open and I walked in and scanned the room. There was an empty seat right next to Phantom and I knew he saved it just for me. Crossing the room, Heat stopped talking and I could feel his eyes piercing my soul, but I ignored his ass and moved faster toward the chair that awaited me.

"I'm glad you decided to join us, Storm." Heat's voice was laced with sarcasm and I loved the way my presence always had him acting out of character. Nodding my head in his direction, I sat and crossed my right leg over my left knee.

"I won't go over what you missed. I'm quite sure someone will fill you in," Heat shot at me. Still, I didn't utter a vowel because I didn't give a fuck. "As I was saying, if Will contacts any of you, hit my line and let me know. It's not like him to go missing."

Missing? What the hell was he talking about? Looking around the room, my eyes landed on Rocko and he had a far-away look in his eyes. If anyone knew where Will was, it would be him. Dreux was sitting with his arms crossed and glaring at Heat like he wanted to attack him. That was the moment I kicked myself for being late to the fuckin' meeting because I was in the dark about what was going on.

"What happened to Will?" I asked out of curiosity.

"Being late is the reason you missed that part of the meeting. Somebody will fill you in on the dynamics." Heat dismissed my question and I didn't like the shit at all. Kayla got my attention and shook her head for me not to go further with Heat. That was too much like right because I needed answers.

"Dreux, tell me what's up, fam."

"Storm! What the fuck did I say to you?" Heat's voice boomed through the room and I swiveled my neck around, ready for war.

"You ain't said shit, nigga! Where the fuck is Will?" I yelled back at his ass. Who the hell did he think he was talking to, Summer? That shit didn't move me and he knew it. "I'm not going to ask again, Heat. This isn't the time to sweep anything under the rug. Especially when it's one of our own. Instead of being in this room, we should be overturning every rock to find Will!"

"Storm, you don't need to be in this meeting. This is my business and being chastised by someone beneath me is not what I'm up for today. Your partner will inform you on the job assignment. I'm not in the mood for your shit. You're the reason we're behind anyway. One more interruption and you will no longer be employed under my belt. As a matter of fact, leave my shit now!"

Heat must've lost his mind if he thought I was going to get up and walk out with my tail tucked under my ass. That was not how I operated. If I was getting put out over my concern for one of our own, this nigga was going to regret the shit. Mark my words.

"Heat, Storm is part of the team. How the fuck you gon' just dismiss her like that?" Dreux asked. "Hell, we've all been asking the same muthafuckin' question, and you have yet to say anything other than he's missing. Why bring the shit up if you didn't have answers, my nigga?"

That's one solid on my side. I was ready to see how things would pan out. I stayed seated to hear what would fall from Heat's lips. When he didn't say anything, I chuckled and crossed my arms over my chest.

"I won't discuss shit until she leaves my muthafuckin' establishment! Since she stepped back on the scene, we've lost out on money. I've come to the conclusion that I no longer want her on the team," he had the nerve to say. "Storm, your services are no longer needed. You can leave on your own free will, or I can forcibly remove you."

The words Heat spoke resonated over and over in my mind. *Did he just fire my ass?* Jealousy was dripping off his tongue like venom from a poisonous snake. This nigga was exposing his pussy in front of everybody because he didn't have probable cause to let me go. I was going to let him have that shit though because I would never beg a muthafucka to allow me to stay where I wasn't wanted.

Slowly rising to my feet, I turned to face Heat and nodded my head. "I'm leaving but remember, you sought me out, not the other way around. I've been put out of better places, Heat. I won't starve without you, nigga. Thanks for the opportunity, just know, there's competition in these streets now. Game on, boo. Let the best one win." I winked at him and turned to leave. Phantom grabbed my hand, pausing me mid-step.

He stood and stared in my eyes for a few seconds before ushering me towards the door. Phantom's gesture surprised me because he was walking away from a job he loved and made lots of money from, for me. I couldn't let him risk his livelihood like that. Snatching my hand out of his grip, I shook my head no.

"Stay, Phantom. Don't walk away from your money. I'm gon' be alright. I will never stay where I'm not wanted," I said lowly.

"Fuck this shit! This nigga movin' shady as fuck and I don't want no parts of it. If you have to bounce, I do too. Now, let's go," he said, taking my hand in his.

"Phantom, if you leave, don't come back when shit gets hard out there for you."

Why in the hell did Heat even open his mouth? Phantom stopped suddenly but he never released my hand. I squeezed his gently and he relaxed a little bit, but that didn't stop him from speaking his mind.

"Nigga, I'm straight with or without you. This ain't my only source of income. What, you thought I was a dumb nigga like some of these muthafuckas that need you? Nah, dawg, far from it. Good luck with keeping this shit afloat."

As we walked out of the door, the sound of chairs and footsteps were heard behind us. Without turning around, I already knew my twin was riding out with me. Khaos wasn't letting Phantom leave alone and Dreux was my nigga if it didn't get no bigger, so I knew he was riding out. Rocko, on the other hand was giving me snake vibes so I didn't expect him to be with me on this one. I had to find out where Will was because he never left without giving word about his whereabouts.

"All you muthafuckas gon' regret walking out!" Heat yelled to our backs. "Storm, I hope that nigga is worth losing everything for!"

I tried to pull away from Phantom to confront Heat, but he basically dragged me away. Rubbing his thumb over the back of my hand repeatedly, I kept moving as we walked through Heat's establishment. The same females that were sitting at the bar when I arrived, stood in the middle of the club floor as we were leaving. Phantom's baby mama stared daggers at us as Summer walked in our direction.

"MaKenzie, can I speak to you for a minute?" she asked, walking a short distance away with a scowl on her face.

Kayla stopped in her tracks and folded her arms over her chest, ready for Summer to get out of her body. Me, on the other hand, wasn't bothered because I had a feeling she was on her Shirley "Woman to Woman" shit. I guess she wanted her feelings hurt, publicly. Dropping Phantom's hand, I followed her a short distance away. Hell, I wanted to hear the bitch out.

"What could we possibly have to discuss?" I asked smugly.

"Heat hasn't been the same since you came back in town. You have taken control of his mind and I want you to stay away from him."

Summer was serious about what she said, but the shit was comical to me and I laughed in her face. She was crazy as hell coming to me about staying away from *her* man. Her issues were with him, not me.

"Hold up. Go back to what you said, Summer. Heat has been acting differently towards *you*. Heat chose to let my presence interfere with how he interacts with *his* woman. Then, you have the audacity to approach *me* with the foolery to stay away from *him*. Nah," I chuckled. "You should be walking to the conference room to confront Heat about all that shit," I said, pointing in the direction her nigga was.

"Kenzie, you know me and Heat is together and you're trying to break us up. I'm not for the bullshit. Just stay the fuck away from him!"

Summer's voice was getting louder with every word she spoke, but it only made her look dumb. Every eye in the building was on the two of us and we were the center of attention. I could be a petty muthafucka when I wanted to be and I chose that moment to put the nail in the coffin. Maybe she would think twice about stepping to me in the future.

"I don't have control over how Heat treats you, Summer. It's obvious that nigga is putting me on the top priority list and you are still an afterthought. Never confront a woman about your man, sweetie. Take that shit up with him. You're trying your best to check me over a man you're madly in love with, but in reality, that nigga loves me. I'm here to tell you, it's one-sided, because I'm done with his ass."

"Stay the fuck away from him, Kenzie! That's the last time I'm going to say it. Take heed to what I said because there won't be any talking next time."

"Is that a threat?" I asked.

"It's whatever you want it to be, Kenzie."

"Aight, bet. From this day forward, I'm no longer Kenzie. When you step to me, address me as Storm. You want to be on bullshit, I'm ready to show you how I handle my enemies," I smirked. "I'll give you a forewarning though, don't bring a knife to a gunfight, lil baby. Bring your whole army, you gon' need it fuckin' with me."

I walked away without another word. Phantom was in a heated conversation with his baby mama and I didn't have time for that nonsense either. I exited the club and headed to my car.

"Kenzie!" Kayla yelled from behind me. I stood next to my car as she quickly approached. "What the fuck was that about?"

"The bitch is sick. Heat's dick got her ass under a spell and I gave her a pass today. The next time she approaches me about him, I'm shooting her between the eyes. Summer must've forgot who the fuck I am. I'm going home to strategize since Heat's pussy ass fired me."

"Sis, you know damn well we don't need him. We will make it together. As for Summer, don't take her ass lightly. I have a feeling there's more to what she said. Keep your eyes open. Have you talked to Nicassy? I've tried calling her and she's not answering."

Thinking about what Kayla said brought me back to the shooting but I shook it off. "No, I haven't spoken to her since she called me a few days ago. She was supposed to be on her way here but I haven't heard anything else from her. You know Nicassy's been on some lowkey shit for damn near a year. She'll call you back eventually."

"That's true, but something is off. I won't think too much into it. Drive safely, sis, and watch your back with Phantom's baby mama too. You're every bitch in a book in there right now." Kayla laughed.

"She knows not to come for me. I've already tapped that ass, she don't want any more problems with the kid. Phantom better give her ass a fair warning and she better take heed. I'm not showing no mercy to these bitches because they're wearing their hearts on their sleeves. Fuck them hoes and the niggas that got them thinking they're super heroes," I said, hitting the button to unlock the doors to my car. I was serious because I wasn't about to allow a bitch to get under my skin about any man.

"Be careful out here, Kayla. Somebody shot at me the other day while I was at Chipotle. I didn't tell you because I didn't want you to worry. Whoever it was got away before Phantom could see who it was."

"What the fuck! You don't fuck with nobody," Kayla said heatedly. "Hell, you be safe out here too. You know all these folks running around on this racial shit. We all have to be careful. It was probably a stupid muthafucka on some random bullshit with black people."

"I don't know what's going on but I'm glad they missed and my eyes are wide open. I want yours to be too."

Giving my sister a hug, I eased into the driver's seat, I started my whip, closed the door and lowered my window. Kayla and I said our goodbyes and I backed out of the parking spot. As I slowly pulled away from the club, Phantom made his exit but I didn't have time for his baby mama drama. My shower and bed were calling me and I couldn't wait to get home.

***

The hot water cascaded down my body and it felt fabulous. Phantom had called as I drove away, asking why I didn't wait for him. I simply responded that I was tired. Heat had pissed me off and on top of all of his shit, Summer wanted to add fuel to the fire. The best place for me was being home alone before I caught a case.

Stepping out of the shower, I grabbed my plush towel from the rack and wrapped it around my body before opening the door to enter my bedroom. The steam followed me out and I screamed, jumping back a little. My brother was sitting on the edge of my bed with his hands clutched together. His locs were freshly done, but something wasn't right and it showed on his face.

"Scony, you scared the shit out of me! What are you doing here?" I asked, making sure the towel was secured against my body.

"I need to talk to you, sis. What I have to say couldn't be delivered over the phone." My brother looked up at me and he had bags under his eyes as if he hadn't slept in days. "I called Kay, but she didn't answer. Have you talked to her today?"

"She should be at home. I saw her not too long ago at the club. We had a meeting and Heat fired my ass." I laughed at the last part because I still couldn't believe how much of a bitch Heat was being. He was deep in his feelings but he would have to figure that shit out on his own.

At the mention of Heat, my brother's scowl was deep as fuck. He pulled his phone from his hip and pressed a button, putting the call on speaker. I took the opportunity to get dressed because standing in front of my brother in a towel was not what the fuck we did in our family. After grabbing a pair of leggings and a t-shirt, I went into the bathroom and slipped on my clothes. When I returned to my room, Scony was still looking pretty down.

"Bro, what's on your mind? It's not like you to pop up out of the blue."

"Kayla is on her way over here. I would rather tell the both of you together, instead of repeating what I have to say. While we're waiting, you can go speak to G. He's in the living room."

"G is here too? Something happened didn't it, bro? Just tell me what's going on. You have me worried."

Hearing his name, G appeared in my doorway. I rushed into his arms and he squeezed me tightly. It was always good to see my brothers, but not when they were holding back information. I knew it was a long stretch, but I had to try my hand with G.

"What's going on, bro?" I whispered loud enough for him to hear.

"Be cool, Kenzie. When Kayla gets here, we will fill y'all in. Until then, feed a nigga." G stepped back rubbing his stomach. I couldn't do anything but shake my head. His ass was always hungry whenever he came around. But I loved him and went into the kitchen to cook some shit up for him and my brother. About an hour later, Kayla had entered my home and G had demolished at least six steak tacos. Scony wasn't hungry but he sat back, sipping a bottle of beer.

"Kenzie, Scony! What's wrong?" Kayla asked as she placed her purse on the coffee table and sat next to our brother, giving him a big hug. G and I walked into the room and sat on the love seat across from my siblings.

"Who is that nigga?" Scony asked, glaring over Kayla's shoulder as he released her.

Following his gaze, I noticed Khaos standing by the door with his hands shoved in his pockets. I jumped up quickly and stood next to him, because I knew how protective Scony was when it came to Kayla and me. As I cleared my voice, Scony and G stood to their full heights and I knew I needed to step in before they started acting like Marcus and Mike in *Bad Boys*.

"Scony, this is Khaos. We all work together." I offered to do the introductions. "Khaos, this is our brothers Scony and G."

"What up?" Khaos said nonchalantly.

"Did yo' mama name you Khaos?" Scony scoffed.

"Nah, but when I don't know a muthafucka, that's what I prefer to be called."

Kayla stood to her feet and turned to Scony. "Look, bro. I'm a grown woman and don't need you to play the big brother role right now. Khaos and I were hanging out when you called and he offered to drive me here. The way you sounded on the phone let me know something was definitely wrong. Now, are you going to stand here grilling him, or are you going to tell us what's going on?"

"Kay, Conte—"

"Fuck Conte! Why are you here, Scony?" Kayla screamed. "That muthafucka's name shouldn't even come up in my presence." She shook her head from side to side as she glared at our brother. I knew the mere mention of Conte would set her off. Scony knew as well, so I didn't know why he even tried that bullshit.

"Kay, come sit down, please. You too, Kenzie," Scony said, shifting to the middle of my sofa. Without a second thought, I sat on the far side of him, but Kayla stayed put. The deep frown on my brother's face softened and he looked like he was close to tears. "When was the last time either of y'all talked to Nicassy?"

It was ironic that Scony asked the exact question Kayla brought up earlier. The pit of my stomach started aching. Something wasn't right, but I wasn't going to jump to conclusions before he could tell us what was going on.

"I spoke with her a few days ago, five days to be exact," I said raising my hand to bite on my stiletto nail. Scony slapped my hand down without looking in my direction.

"Well, I talked to her a few weeks ago and she told me about a job she was assigned to in Houston." He paused as he glanced back and forth between Kayla and me. The confusion on both of our faces must've confirmed what he already knew. We didn't have a clue what he was talking about.

"What assignment? We don't go on any job without one of us knowing about it."

"Kayla, Nicassy informed me that neither of you knew about the assignment, because she was told not to tell anyone. The nigga y'all work for is shady as fuck and sent her on a blank mission. When I confront his ass, he's good as dead," Scony gritted. "Nicassy fell in love with the mark and didn't complete the job." My brother's chin fell to his chest. When he raised his head, tears fell from his eyes.

"What happened to her, Scony?" I yelled, shaking him by the arm.

Wiping his hand down his face, he opened his mouth to speak but nothing came out. My anxiety was on an all-time high because the way he responded let me know there wasn't going to be a happy ending. The mention of Heat only made the situation more puzzling. He was asking about Nicassy as well, so I wasn't understanding what was really going on. Shit wasn't adding up.

"She reached out to me and explained she wanted to tell the mark she was sent to kill him. I told her to pack her shit and leave, she didn't take my advice. Nicassy died five days ago."

Scony choked the last part out, but I heard him loud and clear. I was stunned, but Kayla's cries filled the room and she collapsed to the floor. Khaos was right there to console her. My mind was full of flashbacks, but the last conversation I had with Nicassy kept playing over in my mind. She knew what she'd done and wanted to make amends with me and I blew it off. Now, we would never get the opportunity to reconcile. Even though I still didn't know what caused the riff between the two of us, hearing she died didn't hurt any less.

My body was numb. I couldn't cry, talk, nothing. There was just a tightening in my chest that wouldn't ease up. Hell,

I doubt if I was even breathing. Without warning, I finally broke down.

Meesha

Chapter 10

Khaos

While Kayla was walking to her car after talking to her sister, I rushed to the driver's door before she could close it. There was no way I was going to let her keep running from me. Spending time with her was a must and I was ready to shoot my shot for the second time.

"Hold up, beautiful." I smiled widely and hope it would soften her demeanor. The shit that took place inside the club had her hot as hell. She was even sexier when mad, but that wasn't the way I wanted to see her. "Don't let what went on back there get to you. Whatever Heat is mad at Storm about is weak shit, because he's letting it interfere with business."

"Heat can kiss my ass, Khaos. He lost me and my sister. I'd be damned if I continue to work with his punk ass after that hoe shit he pulled. We don't need that muthafucka. You and Phantom shouldn't have walked out, to be honest. We appreciate y'all riding, but we'll be alright."

"When my cousin left, that was my cue to raise up too. If he don't fuck with a nigga, I don't either. It's a no-brainer, love. Heat's been on some bullshit since y'all came back and I wasn't feeling his vibe. As a matter of fact, things haven't been right before then. I believe there's more going on with him than he's revealing. But just so you know, we got y'all backs."

Phantom stormed out at that precise moment. Kenzie drove out of the parking lot and his eyes followed until she disappeared down the street. His baby mama came crashing out of the club and I knew the drama was about to continue. She pushed Phantom in the back, causing him to stumble a little because he was caught off guard. He swiftly turned around with his fist balled at his sides.

"Tiff, gon' with yo' bullshit! I'm not about to do this with you today," he said, walking away from her.

"You running 'round like you have no care in the world, but all I asked you to do was bring my daughter home!"

"She is at home! We've had this conversation already and you know what you got to do. Until you handle the bullshit at yo' crib, Layla will be with me. There's nothing else to talk about."

Phantom opened the door to his car and Tiffany hauled off and punched him in the side of his head. Why did she do that stupid shit? Fam yoked her up with the speed of lightning. His hand was wrapped tightly around her neck, veins immediately protruded on the side of her forehead.

"I've told you about putting yo' hands on me, bitch! The nigga you need to be fuckin' up, you're not. Me, I'm the wrong muthafucka to run up on. I'll kill yo' ass out here!" he yelled, slamming her head against the side of the car. "This what the fuck you want me do, huh?"

"Let her go, Phan. Don't let her take you out of character. She's showing out for her girls and you falling right into her trap." I was able to get to my cousin before he could put a hurting on Tiffany's ass. Phantom released his baby mama and I pulled her away so he could get in his whip. Phantom cranked his shit up and peeled out.

"Khaos, you always trying to protect his punk ass! Make him bring my baby home!"

"Tiff, you don't think Phantom told me what the fuck going on in yo' crib? What you're going through is not good for Layla. That nigga whoopin' on yo' ass, in front of yo' daughter. She's where she needs to be. You have to get your life together. Phantom is going to take you to court because he don't play when it comes to his child."

"His bitch ass gon' lose too. Fuck you too, Khaos. Y'all not about to dictate what I do with my life! I'm a damn good mother to Layla! It's that bitch that got his ass brainwashed!"

Tiffany snatched away from me and headed toward Kayla's car. I followed behind her and Kayla sat watching everything unfold while waiting for me to return. The door to the club opened and Summer emerged, with Mya on her heels.

"Bitch, I told you when I saw you again it was on sight!" Tiffany screamed while beating on the hood of Kayla's car. "Get the fuck outta the car! You picked the wrong nigga to fuck with and I'm about to whoop yo' ass!"

Tiffany was so fucked up behind Phantom that she didn't realize she was approaching the wrong sister. Running around the back of the car, Tiff was still hollering and Kayla opened the door, but I slammed it shut before she could attempt to get out.

"Go back inside, Tiff. This is not what you want. Your problem is with Phantom, not this woman."

"So, you playing Captain Save-A-Hoe with his bitch now? Fuck that!"

Tiff hawked up a wad of spit and shot it in Kayla's direction. It missed its target but there was nothing I could do when Kayla jumped through the car window like a fuckin' *Power Ranger*. Her little ass had hands that were matched with Mike Tyson himself and Tiff didn't stand a chance. She fucked up when she spit at Kayla because that's the nastiest thing one can do to somebody. She deserved the beatdown she was getting. Kayla slung Tiff on the ground and continuously beat her in the face.

"Bitch, how dare you spit at me! I will kill yo' envious ass! You should've kept that shit funky and went about yo' business!" Kayla transformed before my eyes. She never missed a beat while talking her shit. Every blow connected straight on and there was nothing Tiffany could do about it. She couldn't even cover up.

Tiffany's face was bloody and I had to stop that shit before Kayla, I mean Kane, killed her. She started stomping Tiff in the chest and Summer ran up and pulled her by the hair. Without blinking, Kane handled her ass too. Every punched thrown at Kane, didn't faze her. I seriously believed she had super powers.

Scooping her up my arms, I slung Kane over my shoulder, not knowing she still had Summer by the hair. As I headed to my whip, I could hear Summer screaming with every step I took. Kane was going to work hard on the top of her head. Spinning around only caused Summer to fall to her knees.

"Kane, let her go!"

"She good," Kayla sneered, tossing a handful of her weave in the air. "That was a taste of what you gon' get if you step to my sister, bitch! I'm the mild one and you couldn't hang. Don't come for us, boo."

I walked to my car away from Summer and opened the passenger door. Tossing Kayla into the seat, I hurried to the driver's side and got in, and immediately hit the lock button. Just as I thought, Kayla tried to get out but it wasn't happening on my watch.

"Don't get yo' ass out of this car!" I growled, putting the key in the ignition.

"I have a whole car right there!" Kayla yelled back as she pointed out of the window towards her vehicle.

Ignoring what she said, I backed out of the parking spot as Heat came out of the building. I wasn't trying to get into an altercation with him so I drove off. Kane was fuming but that wasn't my concern at the time. Getting her away from the situation was the only thing on my mind.

"Khaos, turn this muthafucka around or pop the locks, because my car is open to those bitches. My purse is in there as well as my keys! If anything happens to my shit, I'm fucking them up and killin' yo' ass!"

I didn't have a choice but to back up until I was behind Kane's car. Heat was holding Summer in his arms and Tiff was leaning against the building, wiping blood from her face. Glancing over at Kayla, I looked in her eyes and she turned her head, glaring in the direction of the club. She reached for the door handle and I stopped her from pulling it open.

"When I get out, get in the driver's seat and pull off. I will drive your car. Climb over the console, Kayla. Don't get out."

I didn't expect her to do as told, but when I opened the door and stepped out of my vehicle, she climbed into the driver's seat and adjusted it. My cars were my prize possessions and I never let anyone drive them. *She bet not tear my shit up* was the only thing going through my mind. Taking another glance at my whip before crossing the parking lot, I approached Kayla's car and reached for the handle.

"So, you leaving the team with ya boy?" Heat asked while ushering Summer toward the door of the club.

"I'll let you know. You need to get yo' shit in order, Heat. The reason you let Storm go was bullshit. Yo' feelings are fuckin' up yo' judgement and will eventually interfere with yo' business. There is a point where one has to put personal shit to the side and concentrate on what's right for business. For you to be an OG, you're going about this shit all wrong."

"He don't have any feelings for that bitch!" Summer sneered. "She is gone and that's it! Trying to convince him otherwise is pointless."

"Summer, you know the truth and that's why it gets under your skin whenever you see Storm." I laughed, turning to Heat. "Be honest with your woman, man. The game you're playing is dangerous. A woman scorned can be deadly and she's standing right beside you. When shit starts crumbling under your nose, I don't want to be in the line of fire when it takes place. To be honest, you're hiding something and I really don't like the way you're moving, seriously."

"Khaos, I don't need you to tell me what to do. Storm is not the anchor of my business. Remember, she and Kane were gone for two years and my shit was still afloat. The bitch is gone and that's all there is to it. She should've done what I told her to do and she wouldn't be unemployed."

Heat confirmed what I already knew. Storm was let go because of Phantom and again, that was some bitch shit. I wanted to push a little further because I wanted to know what happened to Will. The questions were never answered inside so I was going to try my luck.

"Where's Will?" I asked, leaning against Kane's car.

The shift in Heat's stare didn't go unnoticed to me. He was pretty nervous with my question and tried to hide it. Standing my ground, I focused directly on his eyes and I saw deception before he even opened his mouth.

"I haven't heard from him in days. I'm just as clueless as you are, Khaos. But if you hear from him, let me know and I'll do the same. Actually, you don't work for me anymore, so I don't have to keep you informed on shit. Don't worry about contacting me about what you gon' do, I no longer need your services."

"It's cool. I will *still* call your hoe ass if I hear anything from Will. The only reason you recanted and so-called fired me, is because I'm right about you being shady. You know where one of our own is, Heat. When the truth comes out, you better hope and pray, Will is alive and well or your ass will be on the choppin' block."

I sat in Kane's car and backed out of the parking spot. Pressing on the brake, I let the passenger window down and leaned over so Heat could see my face. "Stay the fuck away from Storm and Kane. The next time those bitches come for them, I promise not to hold them back."

I hit the gas and pulled away from his ass. Glancing in the rearview mirror, Kayla was right behind me. Her ass was a firecracker, and that shit pissed me off and turned me on at the same time. I was going to soften her up sooner than later. The whimpers that would fall from her lips were teasing my mind from the mere thought.

***

Kayla followed me to my house and thought she was just going to park my shit and roll out. Nah, I wasn't ready for her to leave my presence. The incident at the club had her on ten and I used that to my advantage.

"Why don't you come in and calm your nerves? I'm not taking no for an answer though," I said as Kayla walked toward me.

"I just want to go home, Khaos. Those bitches pinched a nerve coming for me like that. The bad thing about it, they thought I was my fuckin' sister! I'm gon' have to tell her to watch out for them hoes. Jealousy is a muthafuckin' sickness."

"See, you're still upset. Just come in for a little bit and we can talk about whatever's on your mind."

"Since you're trying your best to get me to stay, I'll chill with you for a minute. But don't try no sneaky shit. I've already told you what it is with me."

I smiled like a Cheshire cat when she agreed. Leading the way up the walkway, I unlocked the door and stepped aside so she could enter first. Her ass was sitting in her pants just right. My mouth watered at the sight and I imagined cupping both of her cheeks in each of my hands. Picturing myself kissing all over her ass had my dick dancing in my boxers.

"Are you finished molesting me with your eyes?" Kayla asked with a smirk. "You do know, it's not polite to stare at people, right?"

"I-I wasn't staring," I stammered. "Actually, I was out-right lusting and I'm sorry. You are so beautiful and that ass," I said without meaning to as I gripped my bottom lip between my teeth. "I shouldn't have said that and I apologize. But I meant that shit," I said, walking past her to gain entry to my crib.

Kayla shook her head and chuckled lowly as she entered my living room. I closed and locked the door before joining her on the couch. We sat in silence and I felt like a horny ass teenager who brought a girl home for the first time, as if Kayla had never been to my spot. Hell, she cooked in my kitchen.

"You so rude. You're not gonna ask if I want anything to drink? Or are you going to sit there looking crazy?"

Standing to my feet, I laughed because I knew I looked like a lovesick puppy without being able to see the expression on my face. "What would you like to drink, beautiful?"

"A double shot of tequila. Nah, fuck that, bring the whole bottle."

"Do you think that's a good idea? I mean, you still have to drive when you leave here."

"Didn't you ask what I wanted to drink? I'll be fine, Khaos."

I hunched my shoulders as I walked over to the bar. There was still a half bottle of coconut 1800 from the barbeque. The only reason that shit was even in my crib is because that's what the twins requested. Grabbing a shot glass, the bottle of tequila, and a bottled water for myself, I headed back to the couch.

Kayla had kicked off her shoes and got comfortable. I handed her the bottle so she could pour her own poison and sat on the end of the couch where her feet rested. Kayla automatically placed them in my lap as she downed a shot of the alcohol. Filling her glass again, I sat back and caressed the insole of her pretty feet through her socks.

"Mmmmm, that feels good." Her head dropped onto the arm of the couch for a second before she took the second shot to the head.

"I have a question for you. Why are you so against getting to know me on a personal level?" I asked, putting more pressure on her foot.

"I'm not against it at all to be honest," she moaned. The sound alone had me bricked up like a piece of plywood. "I just got out of a very serious relationship and I don't want you to be a rebound of my past. The door must be closed completely before I pursue something new. The way my feelings are set up at the moment, you would be hurt in the long run. I'm never the one to play with anyone's feelings. I'll be straight up with you though, there is a possibility of us getting to know one another. Now just isn't the time."

"I feel you on that and appreciate you clearing it up for me. Kayla, you are a beautiful woman and you deserve to be loved properly," I said, putting more pressure on her feet.

Her eyes rolled to the back of her head but I wasn't trying to turn her on. She took that moment to grab more alcohol and my first thought was to take it from her, but the way her attitude could go from zero to sixty, I decided to let her do what she felt was right. Kayla downed more alcohol and the only sounds were the moans that escaped her lips as I continued massaging her foot.

My tool swelled up with every sound that fell from her lips and I knew it was best if I just stopped. Kayla had other plans. She moved her foot and placed the other one in my hand. The foot I'd already massaged, slid across my manhood and he jumped slightly, causing her motion to still. She took that moment to fill her glass a third time and took the liquid to the head.

"Tell me a little bit about MaKayla," I said, breaking the silence in the room.

"There's not much to tell. I have a twin sister as you know, and an older brother. It's been the three of us since our grandmother passed away a couple years ago. We are originally from Chicago, but we moved here when we were younger. After my grandmother's death, Kenzie and I went back to the Chi with our brother. Shit was hard for all of us. We had trials and tribulations when we went back home, but we got through all of that shit."

"The street life will forever be a part of our world. I don't think there's a way for us to get away from it to be honest." Kayla had a faraway look in her eyes and I knew she and her sister had been through a lot in the past couple years. It kind of explained why the two of them were so hardened on the inside.

"I'm sorry to hear about your grandmother. The bond you and Kenzie have with each other, hold on to that shit, beautiful. There's nothing like having someone in your corner through good and bad. I don't have any siblings, but Phantom is my cousin. He will always be my brother."

Kayla lifted her feet and maneuvered her body so she was straddling my lap. I didn't say a word. I wanted to see how bold she was going to be since she told me not to try no sneaky shit and there she was being just that, sneaky and freaky.

Leaning into me, chest to chest, Kayla ran her tongue along the edge of my ear. I automatically cupped her ass and she grinded slowly on my dick. As she trailed kisses down the side of my neck, I fought hard not to toss her lil ass onto the couch and give her all the lovin' I could muster up. My shit was hard as a rock, but I didn't want to get in too deep while she was under the influence.

Kayla's phone started ringing in her purse and the mood was broken. I reached over and snatched it by the handle from the chair she placed it in and handed the purse to her. She fumbled around until she found it and sighed heavily when it stopped ringing. Before she could react, her phone rang a second time.

"Hey, bro," she said, leaning her head against my chest as she listened. "What are you doing in Atlanta?" Listening some more, she sat up straight. "Okay, I'm on my way. I'll see you in twenty or less." Kayla eased off my lap and sat next to me on the couch as she stuffed her feet into her shoes.

"Everything alright?" I asked, adjusting myself.

"I don't know. My brother is here and he don't just pop up. Something is wrong, because he doesn't sound like himself. He's at Kenzie's house and I need to leave. Thanks for the drink, Khaos. I'm sorry about how I acted today."

I didn't move when she stood, but when she stumbled back into my lap, I knew she couldn't drive. Tipsy is the same as being drunk and that's a no-go for me. She was going to try her best to be combative with me and I was ready for it.

"I'll drive you to Kenzie's. You not in no shape to drive."

"I'm a little tipsy, I'll be alright." I ignored what she said and picked up her purse and keys. Holding her by her hand, I led the way outside to my whip. Kayla paused at the front of her car and I wasn't about go back and forth with her about driving herself. So, I got inside my car after opening the passenger door for her to enter.

After a few minutes, she joined me. I backed out of the driveway and headed to Kenzie's house. The ride was quiet but my mind was on how good Kayla's pussy felt on top of my dick. The thought alone had my shit dancing in my boxers. I glanced over at Kayla and she had her head leaned against the window as she bit into her lower lip. That alone created a visual of how she would look with her legs spread in front of me while we both rode the waves.

Shaking the thought from my head, I concentrated on the road as we neared our destination. Baby girl was really in her feelings and I didn't know what to say to let her know everything was going to be alright. When I pulled into Kenzie's driveway, Kayla was out of my whip before I could put the car in park. Scrambling to catch up with her, I made it to the door after she'd already entered.

When I made my entrance, Kayla was moving around hugging her people, when her brother turned to me and asked who the fuck I was. I introduced myself and he questioned the name I'd given his ass. He didn't know me, and I didn't know him to give my government name. So Khaos is what his ass got.

Kayla went in on him when he brought up the fuck nigga she left in Chicago. The way she checked his ass made my dick hard because Kayla didn't take shit from nobody. One thing I'd learned was that she could hold her own, and wasn't about to let anybody run over her, by no means. Scony finally sat down and let all the irrelevant shit go to get right to the reason he came to Atlanta unannounced.

He asked both of the twins if they heard from someone named Nicassy and then he dropped a bomb by telling them she had died. Kayla collapsed and I was right there to catch her. The sound that escaped her mouth had my heart aching and I knew I had to be there for her. Losing someone close to you could be the hardest feeling for anyone. To see baby girl so vulnerable was something new because she and her sister was so hardcore in the streets.

Kenzie was inconsolable and I had to call Phantom so he could be there for her. I guided Kayla to the nearest chair, bending down so I could look her in the eyes. The tears that fell down her face didn't seem as if they would stop anytime soon.

"I'm going to step outside and make a phone call. I'll be right back, alright?" I said, swiping the tears away with my thumb. Kayla nodded her head but at the same time, she threw her arms around my neck and cried into my chest. There was no way I could leave her in that state, so I wrapped my arms around her and held on for dear life.

"Go make your call, Khaos. I'll be alright," Kayla said releasing the hold she had on my neck.

"Stop crying, beautiful. Things won't be okay anytime soon, but you have to take it one day at a time and I will be right here with you." Kissing her on the forehead, I stood to my full height and walked out the door. Pulling my phone from my pocket, I tapped on Phantom's name and listened to the phone ring a few times.

"What's going on, Cuz?"

"Where you at, fam? I need you to get to Kenzie's crib. She needs you, man."

"What happened to Kenzie?" he asked as he shuffled around with concern in his voice.

"Somebody in her family died and her brother came to tell them about it in person. She's fucked up behind this shit, Phantom. Kayla too."

"Don't go nowhere. I'm on my way." Phantom ended the call and I took a deep breath before going back inside. Kenzie looked up at me and her eyes were bloodshot red from crying. Her hard exterior was nowhere in sight. Scony was talking, but he stopped mid-sentence as I closed the door.

"Khaos, what do you know about this nigga Heat?" he asked. "Did you know Nicassy?"

"Heat is a very private person. Outside of doing jobs for him, I don't know what he's into in his everyday life. We weren't close in that aspect, but I trusted him up until recently. He's been moving funny as fuck and I don't appreciate how he's been coming at Kenzie since she came back on the team. As far as Nicassy, I've never heard the name until today."

"Nicassy is Tornado, Khaos," Kayla said without lifting her head.

"Wait, Tornado is the one that you were asking Heat about and he said he didn't know where she was. So, he lied?" I quizzed.

"According to Nicassy, he sent her on a job and told her to stay quiet about it. She was on the assignment for damn near a year. She fell for the mark which so happened to be my business partner. When I found out Stone's house exploded, I thought he killed her because she came clean about why she really approached him. I have to find out more about this nigga. Is it possible for you to get close to him?" Scony said a mouthful and at that point, I was all in.

Heat was connected to the death of a member of our team and with Will being missing, the current events only solidified my thoughts of him being behind his disappearance. "That may be impossible because when Heat fired Kenzie earlier, my cousin and I walked out right behind her. Dreux stayed behind, but the way shit went down, I believe he's trying to figure out what Heat is on. I'll help anyway I can but we have to figure out a way to get him to talk."

"Dreux left out with us!" Kenzie exclaimed.

"No, he didn't, sis. He turned and went back into the conference room. I didn't see him around when Summer confronted you." Kayla reassured her sister of the fact that Dreux didn't give up his position. Kenzie stood from her seat and glanced around swiftly. Making her way into the back of her home, she came back into the living room with her phone in her hand.

"What's up, Storm?" Dreux's voice bellowed from the speaker.

"Get to my house now! We have shit to discuss."

"Aight, I'm on my way. I was coming to holla at you anyway so we're on the same page. I'll see you in a minute."

Dreux ended the call and Kenzie plopped back on the couch next to her brother and placed her head in her hands. As her shoulders shook, Scony gathered her in his arms and held her tightly. It was going to take a lot to get these two strong women back to the way they were before their world came crashing down on them.

Meesha

Chapter 11

Phantom

Layla and I had a good time shopping and splurging on sweets. By the time we got back to my mother's house, she was knocked out. Spending time with my daughter was the first thing on my mind after leaving the club. The bullshit with Heat, on top of Tiffany being in my face about seeing Layla, weighed heavy on me.

Tiff knew I didn't like my business aired out for everybody to hear, but she called herself confronting me in public and got her ass embarrassed. Putting my hands on her was something I'd never done, but she pushed me to my limit. Luckily, Khaos was there to save her muthafuckin' ass, because I was on the verge of choking her out. She didn't give a damn about seeing Layla, she was more worried about the role Kenzie played in my life.

"What's on your mind, Xavier?" my mom asked, sitting across from me at the kitchen table.

I sat quietly because I really didn't want to relive what I went through earlier in the day. My mama wasn't about to let that shit ride though. She knew everything about my life and I didn't leave her out of the loop on nothing. It was just the two of us, Khaos and my aunt Kimille. We were all we had in this dreadful world because both my mom and aunt were disowned by their families early in life.

"I'm tired of Tiff and the bullshit she's been on. Sorry for my language. She's trying hard to get me to let Layla go back to that house. I'm not going, Ma. That nigga beating her ass and she's constantly lying about being with his ass. Layla isn't about to be subjected to all that domestic shit she got going on. I have to think about my daughter first at all times."

"You are absolutely right about that, son. I'm not against anything you're doing when it comes to Tiffany, but I want you to get in touch with Chanel soon as possible and go about it the right way. Don't keep telling her what you're going to do, take action! The longer you prolong the situation, the more she's going to think you're all talk."

"I know, Ma. I'm going to contact Chanel in the morning. Layla belongs with me."

"Good, because I would hate for her to push you over the edge, and you do something you will regret. I raised you not to put your hands on any woman, but I know how Tiffany is. She would provoke until you wring her damn neck."

"Yeah, she took me there and she was lucky Cuz was there to pry my hands from around her neck. When she hit me, I lost my cool."

"Next time, call me. I'll whoop her ass for you. Don't fall into her trap, Xavier. Layla needs you free to spend time with her physically. If you're locked away for beating her mama's ass, that will crush my grandbaby and me."

My mama got up and went to the fridge and grabbed a bottled water. "You want anything out of here?" she asked.

"Nah, I'm good." Tapping my knuckles on the table, my mama sat back in the same chair she vacated moments before. The way she stared at me intensely told me she knew I had more on my mind. It was time for me to make my exit before she got too deep in my business.

"Sit your ass down! You're always bottling shit up, then in the long run, you end up doing something stupid. What else is going on, Xavier?"

Sighing heavily before I sat back in the chair, I looked at my mama knowing I couldn't lie to her. "One of the dudes I work with is missing. I believe Heat knows what's going on with the situation. The fact that he's not saying much, is telling me a lot. And the way Heat keeps coming at Kenzie is starting to piss me off."

"What's his problem with Kenzie?" my mama asked after taking a sip from her water bottle.

"He's a bitch!" I yelled out. "Sorry for my language, but he is acting like a young ass punk because she doesn't want to fu—be with him anymore. Hell, he has a woman and still trying to pressure Kenzie to be alone until he decides to entertain her with his presence. Who would want to live their life that way?"

"He's a damn fool. I know you have some type of feelings for Kenzie, Xavier. You have a lot to do with the way he's acting out. Heat is intimidated by you, because a blind man can see the two of you have a spark between y'all. There's no telling what he may do, son. I want you to be careful out there."

I wasn't worried about Heat doing anything to me, but Kenzie was the one I was worried about. The only thing I could do was watch her back and make sure that nigga didn't catch her slipping. I didn't think he was crazy enough to do anything to her, because he would have to answer to not only me, but the rest of the crew too.

"Ma, I can handle Heat if it comes to that. I doubt it though."

My phone vibrated in my pocket and I stood to retrieve it. Looking down at the screen, Khaos' name was on display. I answered without hesitation and when he told me Kenzie needed me, I wasted no time to get to her. After getting off the phone with my cousin, I turned to my mama and kissed her on her cheek.

"I have to go. There's a death in Kenzie's family and I need to go make sure she's good. I'll be back later to get Layla.

Under no circumstances is Tiff allowed to take her out of this house. If she shows up, call me right away."

"Xavier, please don't do anything irrational out there. Avoid all trouble and if you need *me,* you better find a way to call. Be careful, son. I love you."

The worry in my mama's eyes hurt my heart. I knew she worried about me every time I was out of her sight. She and Layla were the reason I grind so hard, to make sure neither one of them would ever want for anything. Working for Heat has been good, but that's not where my financial status ends. Both Khaos and I have businesses to fall back on. Being a hitman was never our permanent plan.

Leaving my mama's house, I jumped in my whip and backed out of the driveway like a madman. Kenzie didn't let me in on her personal life, so I wouldn't be able to feel anything for the family member she lost. All I knew was I had to be there for her. The silence in the car was smothering a nigga so, I reached over and pushed the button to turn on the radio. It didn't matter what was on, long as the silence was eliminated.

I made the trip to Kenzie's house in less time than it would usually take and ended up parking on the street. Getting out of my car, another vehicle pulled alongside me. My hand automatically went to my Glock and I pointed that muthafucka directly at the driver. The window came down and I was staring in Dreux's eyes.

"Calm down, nigga. It's just me," he laughed.

"Fuck you doing here?" I asked, putting my tool back in place.

"Kenzie called me. I was already on my way over here before she hit my line. Let me park my shit and we can go in together."

I leaned inside my car and retrieved the blunt out of my armrest. Flaming up, I waited patiently for Dreux to get out of his whip. As I hit the blunt, I damn near choked because the smoke went down wrong. I coughed until tears fell from my eyes but that didn't stop me from hitting that muthafucka again once I got myself together. Spitting on the ground, I wiped my mouth as Dreux walked up on me.

"I saw you over here coughing up a lung, nigga. Thought I was gon' have to call the bambalance for your ass," Dreux laughed.

"Fuck you! I was over here dying and yo' monkey ass taking yo' time getting to me. It's all good though, I already know you ain't shit, so it don't matter."

"You good, fool. On some real shit, what's going on with Kenzie? She sounded pissed when she called me."

"Truthfully, I don't know. Khaos called and said there was a death in the family and both Kenzie and Kayla are fucked up about it. I came to see what's going on myself. Hell, I don't think he even told her I was on my way," I said, hitting the blunt a couple times before tossing it into the street.

We walked toward the crib together and I rang the doorbell. Stuffing my hands in my pockets, I waited patiently for someone to come open the door. As I reached to push the doorbell again, it swung open. A nigga with long dreads stood before me with a mug on his face.

"Who the fuck are you?" he barked.

"Where's Kenzie?" I shot back, ignoring the way he approached me.

"You didn't answer my muthafuckin' question!"

"Scony, don't answer my damn door like that!" Kenzie shouted from inside the house. "It ain't nobody but Dreux. Now let him in!"

Moving to the side, the dude I assumed was her brother allowed me and Dreux to enter. As I moved in the direction of Kenzie's voice, she wasted no time going off without looking up from the blunt she was rolling. The way she snapped let me know she wasn't expecting me to be in her home. She directed her words at Dreux.

"Explain why you didn't have my back today at the club, fam." The way Kenzie licked the wood made my joint jump excitedly in my pants, but I knew it wasn't the time to think about sex. Turning slightly, I adjusted my shit as I walked further into the room.

"I had your back one hunnid percent," Dreux responded as he sat down in the nearest chair to the door. "All of y'all walked the fuck out without getting any answers to the questions asked. One of us had to stay behind to see what Heat's ass is hiding. Don't ever pan me out to be a snake muthafucka, Kenzie. You know I'm solid as they come."

"What did you find out?" she asked, finally looking up from what she was doing. Kenzie's eyes landed on me and she dropped her spiff onto the carpeted floor. "Phantom, I didn't know you were here." I nodded my head but my eyes were on Dreux, waiting for him to tell us what Heat had to say.

"Hold up, I don't want to discuss shit until somebody tell me who the fuck this nigga is."

"Scony, Phantom. Phantom, this is my brother Scony. Dreux, let me hear it," Kenzie said, dismissing the bullshit her brother was on.

"What you not gon' do is shut me the fuck up, Kenzie! Who is this nigga to you?" Scony demanded to know.

Kenzie stood from where she sat and looked at her brother angrily. I didn't want her arguing with her brother, because there were other pressing issues, other than finding out who I was. Before she could address him, I put my hand up to stop what I was sure to become an outright argument. Khaos raised up and so did another guy that was sitting on the loveseat with his hand on his waistline.

"Everybody calm down," Kayla said, standing as well. "This shit going in another direction and it's uncalled for. Phantom is cool and his relationship to Kenzie is irrelevant," she said, turning to Scony. "Bro, I know you are concerned about our wellbeing, but we are grown. You have to come out of big brother mode and concentrate on the problem itself. Nicassy is dead! Finding out what happened to her should be the only thing to worry about."

What Kayla said was true and I wanted to clear the air on my part so Scony would be at ease. If I was in his position and someone in my family was killed, I would protect them at all costs. I turned to Scony and held my hand out for him to shake, but he looked at it like I had shit on my fingertips. Clearing my voice, I formally introduced myself while he stared daggers through my body.

"I'm Xavier Bennett, better known as Phantom in the streets. I've worked briefly with your sisters before we all walked out on Heat earlier today. My cousin Khaos hit me up and told me Kenzie needed me, because someone close to her had passed away. I'm here to make sure she's good. Nothing more, nothing less."

"I don't trust nobody that worked under Heat! He had something to do with my sister dying and everybody in his camp is on my radar," Scony barked. "Far as I know, all you muthafuckas knew what the fuck was going on and left Kenzie and Kayla in the dark about the shit!"

"Hold up! Kenzie, Kayla, and Nicassy was like family to me!" Dreux added. "Now, I see why you are screening everybody, and I respect that shit. Let's just settle down and get the story about what went on with Tornado so we can all be on one accord."

I listened while Scony filled us in on what he knew about Tornado's death. I remembered Heat asking Kenzie if she'd heard from her, but I didn't know they were family. Heat had never mentioned Tornado to me personally so, I didn't know her at all. My mind was boggled from what I was hearing because it let me know off back, Heat couldn't be trusted.

"Nicassy told me firsthand that Heat sent her on the job. Y'all work for a grimy ass nigga that has been keeping all of y'all out of the loop of what's going on in his operation. I bet he's been blaming my sisters as the reason he doesn't have work for y'all too, huh?"

"How did you know that, bro?" Kayla asked stunned.

"Heat is not the person that gets the jobs to dish out to y'all. Stone is," G said, taking over the conversation. "Heat's plan was for Nicassy to eliminate Stone so he could take over. When that didn't work in his favor after Nicassy fell in love, the bastard put a hit out on both of them. He fucked up because the job was botched and Stone lived. I don't want a word of this to leave this room. We are the only ones that know the dynamics of what happened and I want to keep it that way."

"Dreux, you said you stayed behind because you basically have suspicions about ya boss, correct?" G asked.

"Yeah. His ass is moving real slimy. When he fired Kenzie for no reason, I knew there was a story behind his bullshit. Unfortunately, I didn't learn anything new while I was there. Heat left after the altercation between Kayla and Tiff. He entered the club going off on Summer, but basically dismissed us."

"I'll tell you about it later. That shit not even important," Kayla responded as Kenzie stared at her from across the room.

"Aight, I need you to keep close tabs on him. If he moves, you move. I want to know every step he takes and if he is planning on leaving Georgia at any given time. As a matter of fact, I want to know everything, down to who the nigga is fuckin!" G stated.

"I can give you the run down on him. I'll send it to you in an encrypted email," Kenzie spoke up. "G, I can be the person to get close to Heat."

"No!" Both Scony and I objected to that idea immediately. Kenzie frowned at the two of us and rolled her eyes. Scony's intense gaze went back and forth between Kenzie and me. At that moment, he realized there was more between us than we revealed. Hell, I'd tell his ass straight up that I knew how his sister's sugary walls felt. Or how her pussy tasted like a sweet Georgia peach. Scony was their big brother, he wasn't shit to me. Scony didn't say what was on his mind but instead, he shook his head.

"He's going to see right through that shit, Kenzie. Heat just fired you earlier. That would be stupid of me to allow you to go at him under false pretenses," I said calmly.

"He fired me because he can no longer get the pussy. All I have to do is ease his mind and pretend I made a mistake. He would melt like butter in my hands."

"That's bullshit, Storm! You ain't doing it, case closed." I raised my voice at her, before turning my attention across the room. "Dreux, you are in charge of finding out what Heat's plan is. I have a feeling Loco knows something. I can pick his brain without making him suspicious. We need to keep an eye on Rocko too. He was fidgeting every time Will's name was mentioned. I didn't put two and two together until I heard Scony's story about Tornado. Rocko was unreachable for a day not too long ago. I don't know if there's a connection, but we can't let it go unnoticed."

"I think you're on to something. Rocko and Will is close as hell. For him, it's unusual that he didn't have anything to say as far as where Will could be. In my gut, he may know exactly where Will is. I have an eerie feeling Will may be dead." Dreux took his phone out and made a call, but hit the end button when the person didn't answer.

"Will's still not answering."

"I'm hoping they didn't kill the big homie. He stood ten toes down with Heat too. The saying goes, 'you have to watch the people closest to you harder than the people that's against you' and it's a damn shame," I said, closing my eyes briefly.

The thought of Big Will being dead was fucking with me on a different level. He was a mentor to all of us, seeing he was an OG and wanted us all to be on our shit. I was trying to figure out what reason Heat would have to kill him. It wasn't ringing a bell at the moment, but I was sure it would surface sooner than later.

Chapter 12

MaKayla

Even though Nicassy stopped talking to me because of her fallout with my sister, it hurt badly when Scony revealed she was killed. Kenzie broke down but put her hard outer-shield back in place when Heat's name was mentioned. The hurt was replaced with revenge in a blink of an eye. My sister was going to go after Heat on her own and there would be nothing anyone could do to stop her.

The guys exchanged numbers after running down the game plan. I just wanted to go home and crawl under the covers and cry. Scony informed us he would be in town for a few days, because he had to be back in Chicago to retrieve Nicassy's body. Burying my sister wasn't something I was looking forward to. The thought alone took me back to the very day I had to do the same for my grandmother, and it was a rough time for me.

"I'm going to get out of here. Scony, I'll get up with you tomorrow sometime. I just want to go home and get in the bed."

"Kayla, be careful. If you need me, give me a call. I'm staying at the Hyatt so I'm not going to be too far away."

"Scony, you didn't have to get a hotel room. Both Kenzie and I have plenty of room for you and G."

"The way it looks, y'all need privacy," he said with a frown.

I wasn't about to go down that road with his ass again, so I didn't even respond. Instead, I glanced over at Khaos and he rose up and headed for the door. Making my rounds, I gave everybody a hug and walked to the door to make my exit.

"Kayla," Scony said from the couch. I turned in his direction and he smiled. "I love you."

"I love you too, bro."

Once Khaos and I exited the house and closed the door behind me, my eyes started watering as I thought about the news my brother bestowed upon us. I fought hard not to drop a tear, especially in the presence of Khaos. He waited patiently for me while holding open the passenger door of his car. I walked slow as hell trying to compose myself before he could see that I was on the verge of crying a river.

"Are you okay?" he asked as I neared.

Nodding my head yes, I hurried and sat in the seat while using the seat belt as the reason to turn away from him. Speaking was the last thing I wanted to do. My throat was burning from struggling not to break down. Knowing I would never hear Nicassy's voice again tugged at my soul. We did so much together growing up and it bothered me that much more, because I didn't get the chance to say goodbye, or even I love you.

I placed my head against the window and closed my eyes. The car shifted as Khaos sat in the driver's seat. I could feel him staring at me but I refused to glance in his direction. Once he realized I wasn't going to acknowledge him, the engine finally purred to life and he backed away from Kenzie's house.

The silence was deafening inside of Khaos' car and I hoped he would turn on the radio, but he never did. Images of Nicassy and me danced behind my lids, forcing me to open my eyes and watch the scenery as we sped on the highway. Khaos grabbed my hand from my lap and gave it a gentle squeeze. I couldn't muster up the energy to pull away from him. His touch was actually what I needed because a sense of calm fell over me.

A lone tear escaped my right eye and rolled down my cheek. I discreetly wiped it away and became upset because I hated to cry in front of people. Khaos lifted my fingers to his lips and kissed each one as he continued to drive.

"You don't have to be strong around me, Kayla. If you want to cry, do that shit. Holding in pain is never good for anybody. That shit drains your energy, baby girl. Tornado will be walking beside you every day from this point on. She's your guardian angel and will forever live in your heart. I'm here long as you need me. You have to let that shit out. Hoarding the feelings can destroy you."

I didn't respond, but he spoke words of truth. Sniffing to prevent the mucus from escaping my nose, Khaos leaned slightly toward me and opened the glove compartment. Handing me a few napkins, I thanked him lowly and blew my nose. It sounded as if I was blowing a bullhorn and Khaos laughed, which caused me to chuckle a little bit.

"That's what I want to see, your smile."

As quick as the words left his mouth, the smile fell from my face. Thoughts of Heat's involvement entered my mind and disrupted my peace; again. Khaos wanted me to express my feelings and I was ready to do just that, but it had nothing to do with the death of my family.

"If Heat had anything to do with what happened to Nicassy, he's going to die brutally! Every time her name was mentioned, his ass acted as if he had no clue of her whereabouts. Hearing my brother say Nicassy told him Heat sent her on a job, blew my mind. Me nor my sister knew anything about that. It was unusual for any of us to take an assignment without informing one another."

"Heat is wrapped up in this, Kayla. There are no ifs, ands, or buts about it. He may not have done the shit himself, but that nigga orchestrated it. It's not a coincidence that Nicassy died and the man she was sent to kill ended up in the hospital. We gon' have to weed out the other niggas involved. I have a couple of names I'm going to check into, but I won't disclose my suspicions just yet."

Khaos thought he had shit figured out but I was ten steps ahead of him. My sister was dead and the minute I was told, the wheels started spinning. We didn't know all the details, but I knew enough to know there were snakes in the operation we trusted with our lives.

"Khaos, I'm not stupid. Los is one of the people on my radar because I knew something was up with him from day one. He's definitely going to slip up and sign his own death certificate. You've worked with him, I'm going to need you to tell me all about his ass." I shifted in the seat so I could see his reaction to what I'd said.

"Yeah, I'm heading in the right direction," I smirked. "Rocko is moving like his name, Rocky as fuck! See, I know him well. He was around when Kenzie and I were just baby assassins. He's a very vocal nigga. Rocko didn't say shit in that meeting today! Will and Rocko is thick as thieves. Not once did he question Heat about Will. Thinking back on it, Rocko was mute the entire time. The only thing that moved was his shifty ass eyes. So, you don't have to disclose what I've already peeped."

Khaos nodded his head in agreeance with a slight smile. "You and your sister don't miss a beat, I like that. I won't be able to stop y'all from doing whatever the two of you are going to do. All I ask is for you to keep me and Phantom in the know. The last thing I want is for y'all to try to handle shit on your own. Before you try to object, I'm not saying y'all can't, I just want you to know that you don't have to handle it alone. Heat is clever, Kayla. We have to go into this as if we don't suspect anything at all. Can you promise me that much?"

Contemplating Khaos' question as he slowly turned into his driveway, it didn't take long for me to come to a conclusion. I could've said what he wanted to hear, but I'm a real one. I'll never say anything I really didn't mean.

"I can't make a promise that I know for a fact I won't keep. One thing's for sure, I'll fill you in, but I'm fuckin' shit up on sight and I may not have time to inform you beforehand," I replied, hunching my shoulders.

Soon as Khaos stopped, I damn near ran to my car. He walked over to my window as the engine purred to life, staring at me until I rolled it down. "Are you good to drive?" he asked.

"Yeah. I'm no longer sad, I'm pissed right about now. It will simmer down once I'm in the comfort of my own home. If it makes you feel better, I'll call you when I get there."

I forced a smile but I was sure it didn't reach my eyes. My heart was screaming for me to release the pain harboring in my chest. Sympathy was the last thing I wanted anyone to have for me. Hiding my emotions was a must in the profession I was in.

"Okay, I'm going to take your word on that. Make sure you hit my line because I'll be waiting for your call."

Khaos walked toward his house slowly but looked back at me several times. I shifted the gear into reverse and backed up just a little bit before the dam broke. Lowering my head, I pretended to look for something when Khaos paused on his porch. Clearing my voice, I yelled out to him.

"I'm good, go in the house!"

Doing as I asked, he opened and shut the front door. I threw the gear in park and let the tears flow down my face. It felt as if I was hyperventilating and couldn't catch my breath. The pain in my chest was unbearable and I hadn't felt that type of pain since my granny passed away. A piece of me died along with Nicassy and I knew it would be a long time before I came back from it.

***

As I turned over in the bed, I opened my eyes but it was dark. I never slept in complete darkness when I was home alone. Alarm bells rang in my head because for one, I didn't remember driving out of Khaos' driveway. Secondly, the bed wasn't mine because the mattress felt as if it was hugging my body with precision. Thirdly, there was a masculine scent invading my nostrils and there shouldn't be any man in my shit.

Swinging my legs from the bed, I stood, trying to figure out where the hell the light switch was. I bumped into something hard and yelped out in pain. Rubbing my hip, I heard footsteps getting closer to the room and I was pissed because somebody caught my ass slipping and kidnapped a bitch. I grabbed the first thing I could get my hand on and waited for the door to open. I was ready to jab a muthafucka's eyes out of their head.

The footsteps got closer and I backed up behind the door as it crept open. A dark figure walked in, flipped the light on in the process, and I raised the object in the air to attack. Lunging forward, I stopped mid swing with my arm in the air and Khaos bent over, laughing his ass off.

"What the fuck were you going to do with that, Kayla?" He asked pointing at my hand laughing.

Glancing up, I couldn't do nothing but join in on the laughter. I was holding a damn back scratcher for protection. What type of damage was I going to do with that shit? Out of all the things in the world I could've grabbed, a damn back scratcher was what I ended up with.

"Look, I grabbed the first thing I put my hand on, nigga! Waking up in the dark, in an unknown location, scared the shit out of me," I said, putting the back scratcher on the dresser. Khaos stared at me for a few seconds before I turned away from him and sat on the edge of the bed. "How did I end up in your bedroom?"

Khaos never took his eyes off me as he leaned against the door frame. "After entering the house, I thought you had pulled off since you were backing out of the driveway before I closed the door. But when I went to the kitchen and just so happened to look out the window, I saw you were still sitting at the end of the driveway with the car running. You had been out there maybe twenty minutes and your head was slumped oddly to the side. I rushed out thinking you were dead. I carried you inside and called a doctor that worked for us to check you out."

What Khaos said had me thinking back to when I was in the car. I remember crying, but nothing afterwards. "What did this so-called doctor say?" I asked curiously.

"He said you were just exhausted and in shock from the news you received. When he left, I took you to my room to rest. I hope that wasn't a problem."

"No, obviously I needed it. Waking up in an unfamiliar place just scared me. I'm hungry as hell though. I'm going to leave so I can grab something to eat before going home."

"I cooked something earlier. Do you want me heat up a plate for you?"

Nodding my head yes, I watched Khaos as he left the room. Looking around his bedroom for my purse, I spotted it on the nightstand next to the bed. As I reached inside, my phone started ringing. Conte's name displayed on the screen and I sighed loudly before accepting the call.

"Yeah."

"Kayla, where the fuck are you? Scony said you left Kenzie's house to go home hours ago and I've been sitting in front of your house for an hour and you ain't here!"

I pulled the phone away from my ear and wiggled my finger around inside my ear canal before responding. I had to make sure I heard this nigga correctly because he must've lost his mind questioning me. Last I checked, we were no longer connected.

"Why are you at my house, Conte? As a matter of fact, why the fuck are you even in Atlanta?"

"What you mean? I came to make sure you were okay. Nicassy meant a lot to all of us, Kayla. I'm affected by her passing too."

Conte was trying to use Nicassy's death to his advantage, but little did he know, that shit wasn't going to get him anywhere with me. Running down here was a waste of time for him because I didn't need nor want him to console me. When I said I was done, I meant that shit. He didn't comprehend the logic behind it though.

"We all are hurting, Conte. That doesn't explain why you are sitting outside my crib and questioning me like you are my nigga. Go back to Chicago," I said nonchalantly.

"Tell me where you are. I'll—"

"I'm not telling you shit! Go home and stop trying to figure out my whereabouts. You already know where I'm not and that should've told you to move the fuck around. I have nothing more to say to you. We are done. I don't want you worrying about me because I'm good. Now, leave me alone! I'm not gon' ask again, this is me being nice."

"Kayla, I fucked up and I'm sorry. I want us to work shit out. A nigga miss you, damn!"

Conte could talk until he was blue in the face, I wasn't hearing that shit. Khaos was heading my way and I didn't give a damn. Conte was still talking on the other end of the phone but I wouldn't be able to repeat what he was saying because I'd tuned him all the way out. The aroma of whatever Khaos cooked hit my nostrils and my mouth watered with anticipation.

"I didn't give you much, but there's enough for you to get full," Khaos explained as he set up the portable dinner table in front of me.

He placed the plate down and my eyes scanned the food with delight. Khaos made lasagna, garlic bread, sweet peas and a salad. Seeing the food made me forget Conte was still on my phone. Boy, he was pissed.

"Who the fuck is that?" Conte yelled, bringing my attention back to the phone.

"None of your business. Look, I'm about to eat. I won't be coming to my house tonight so don't waste another minute of your time waiting for me. Goodbye, Conte." Ending the call before he could respond, I tossed my phone onto the bed and picked up the fork to taste the lasagna. "Mmmm, this is so good. Do you have parmesan cheese?" I asked, taking another bite.

"Yeah, I'll get it for you," Khaos said, leaving the room for the second time. My phone chimed and a text came through. Wiping my hands on the napkin Khaos brought with my plate, I picked up my phone.

Conte: That nigga is the reason you're giving me the cold shoulder! That shit is foul, Kayla. All you had to do was tell me you were fuckin' with someone else, instead of bringing up shit I did in the past.

Me: If you think another man is the reason I told you to fuck off, you're sadly mistaken. You and I are no longer because of YOU! The bullshit I was holding in just so happened to come to play after your stupid ass ultimatum. We've been done, Conte. I just didn't want it to be. But now, I don't give a damn about you and whatever you have going on in your life. To set the record straight, I have friends that you know nothing about and no, I'm not fuckin' them. That may change though, muthafucka.

Conte: Kayla, come home so we can talk.

Me: Fuck you! Go back to Chicago!

Conte continued to text, but I ignored every one of them because I wasn't about to go back and forth with him. My phone rang as I bit into my garlic bread and Khaos entered the room with the parmesan cheese. I smiled as I answered the phone for Kenzie.

"Sis, where the hell are you? Conte is at your house!" she yelled in my ear.

"I know he's at my house but that's his choice, I didn't invite him. He's been blowing my phone up and that's not going to make me change my mind. If anything, it's pissing me off. To answer your first question, I'm at Khaos' house."

"You've been there since y'all left here?" Kenzie was smiling for sure because her voice changed from loud to angelic-like. "Oh shit, you been doing the nasty," she laughed.

"No, I haven't, bitch. I just might though. My food is getting cold so I'll talk to you later or tomorrow. I'm turning my phone off, so Conte may hound you when he can't reach me."

"Aht-Aht! Block that nigga or something, but keep your phone on. There's too much going on for me not to be able to get in touch with you. Tell Khaos not to break your back too much, we have some running around to do tomorrow. I will come over with clothes and shit, so you don't have to go home first. I'll make sure to call ahead of time."

"Alright. That sounds like a plan. I love you, sis."

"I love you too, Kayla."

I put the phone down and shook the cheese onto my lasagna. Concentrating hard on getting just enough cheese, I didn't realize Khaos was still standing next to me until it was too late. He folded his hands over his chest and the movement caught my attention.

"What?" I asked, looking up at him while continuing to shake the container.

"That's a lot of damn cheese, Kayla."

"You sound like my damn sister right now. To be honest, it's not enough," I laughed.

"There's more cheese than pasta at this point. Give me that!"

Khaos snatched the cheese from my grasp and I dug into the meal. The shit was so good, I wanted more but I was ashamed to ask. I didn't want him to think I was a pig. There was still a pile of peas on the plate, along with a whole piece of bread. I couldn't eat them without more lasagna.

"You want more lasagna? I have plenty more," Khaos asked, reading my mind.

"Sure, if you insist." I smiled, holding the plate out to him. "Bring a cocktail back with you. Tequila and pineapple juice please. Oh, and a bottled water."

"How about you come downstairs? After you eat, I know you gon' want to smoke."

That was right up my alley. Staying in the bedroom wasn't good, because I didn't want to let on that I wanted Khaos to feel on my booty. I'd let that play out on its own since I had no plans of going home. Conte was big mad about me being in the presence of another nigga, but he had opened the door for me to have some much-needed fun to take my mind off everything.

An hour later, I was full of the food I'd eaten and higher than a muthafucka. The tequila I'd consumed didn't make matters any better. Khaos inquired about my relationship with Conte and I filled him in. It was pretty cut and dry, but it felt good to talk about the situation. When he told me about his ex, I tried hard not to roll my eyes because I hated a bitch that took a man's kindness for weakness.

His ex-girlfriend used him for what he could do for her then got caught cheating in the home they shared. The way Khaos and Phantom rolled, it surprised me when he said he left and never looked back. I was waiting on the part of the story where he choked that bitch and shot the nigga. Ain't no way both of them would've walked out of that crib. It would've been staged as a murder-suicide had it been me.

I changed the vibe and had Khaos put on some music. We rapped, sang, danced, and just enjoyed each other's company for a spell. When his playlist switched to slow songs, my yoni started tingling and I was on my fourth cocktail. They say the third one was a charm, but the fourth was gonna do harm—to my kitty.

Khaos pulled me from the couch and I spilled a little bit of my drink. Downing the remainder of the tequila, I placed the glass on the coffee table before stepping into his awaiting arms. The man only wanted to dance with me but I wanted more than that. In my mind, it was freaky time and I wanted it. As he wrapped his arms around my waist, the sultry tunes of *Teddy Pendergrass* set the mood for me. It was just a dance to him, but it was all sexual for me.

Running my hand up the back of his wife beater, the ripples of his muscles felt good in my palms. I closed my eyes and breathed in his masculine scent. The *Creed* cologne was kind of like a sexual euphoria for me. My lady parts were tingling out of control. The smell of a man has never gotten me riled up, ready to fuck. But there was a first time for everything.

My hands went from his back to the inside of his pants. Khaos broke the hold on my waist and took a couple steps away from me. He clasped my hands in his and stared deeply in my eyes.

"Kayla, what are you doing?" Khaos asked breathily.

I couldn't answer his question verbally because his actions screamed rejection and I felt stupid for trying to force intimacy onto him. From the start, I turned the man standing in front of me down, but I needed him at that precise moment. The way he stared at me said a lot but I didn't know exactly what. Getting down on his knees so we were face-to-face, I took the opportunity to passionately kiss his full lips.

"If we go through with this, there's no turning back," he said, pulling away from the kiss. "I'm not the one to fuck *any* woman. If that was the case, I would've had my share by now. Once I dip in the pot, that shit belongs to me. So, I want you to think about this before we take things any further."

Think about if I wanted dick? This muthafucka was out of his mind. There was nothing to consider about the subject. Instead of responding verbally to his little speech, I reached out and grasped his pants. Lowering them slowly over his hips, along with his boxers, I watched his joint spring out and it was beautiful. The thickness of his member had me clenching my love muscles tightly.

My mouth watered and I couldn't wait another minute to devour his chocolate stick. Without lifting a finger, I kissed the tip and ran my tongue along the underline of his shaft. I could've sworn his head wink at me, that's all it took for me to give Khaos my best oral performance. Relaxing my throat, I massaged his meat with my jaws and swallowed him whole.

"Shit!" Khaos growled, pulling a handful of my hair. "Fuck, Kayla!"

Drool escaped the side of my mouth and made it much easier for me to glide his dick in and out. I gagged as the tip hit the back of my throat and my eyes closed automatically, but that didn't stop me from putting in work. I used both hands, jerking his dick fast. The movement had him moaning loudly and I felt every vein in the palm of my hand.

Khaos stepped out of my grasp and there was a loud popping sound when his shaft was released from my lips. "I'm not ready to cum just yet. I want you to cum all over this dick. Plus, I can't go out like that, you almost had me screaming out like a female."

In one swift motion, Khaos lifted me off the floor and into his arms. He carried me toward the stairs as he kicked his pants and boxers from around his feet. The struggle was real and he tripped soon as we reached the carpeted stairs. He placed his hands behind my head before the impact could hurt me. Instead of lifting me again and continuing our journey, Khaos removed my pants and buried his head between my legs.

Caressing my watery treasure with his tongue, the arch in my back was deep. I felt the stress leaving my body instantaneously. Khaos expertly kissed my lower lips as I grabbed a handful of his locs and pulled him further into my kitty. I rotated my hips to a song only I could hear and the video was playing in real time before me.

My stomach constricted tighter than a snake suffocating its prey. I took a deep breath and allowed my love secretions to flow down his throat. Khaos was thirsty because he wouldn't let up, causing me to scream out in ecstasy. Wiping his hand across his mouth, Khaos wasted no time climbing between my legs. He leaned forward and guided his meat into my sacred honey pot.

Slowly maneuvering in and out of my kitty, I felt my juices gliding between my ass cheeks. Khaos placed both of his forearms under my thighs and brought them over my head. His strokes became very aggressive and I loved that shit. My body was balled up like a WWE wrestler pinned to the mat.

"Oh shit! Yes, hit that shit, Khaos." I was trying my best not to yell out but the way his dick bounced off my walls, there was no way to suppress it.

"This is my pussy now, Kayla," Khaos groaned. "Fuck that, you belong to me. You just sealed the deal, baby."

We were fucking wildly, right on the steps of his home. That shit felt so right. At that moment, I didn't want to be anywhere else. But I didn't think I'd be able to promise Khaos the commitment he was looking for.

Chapter 13

Heat

Summer's been on my ass since the shit went down at the club. She swore up and down, me and Kenzie were still fuckin' around, but she was far from the truth. Kenzie wanted nothing to do with me and it had a lot to do with that nigga Phantom. The way he marched his ass out of the meeting behind her let me know he was the one fuckin' her good. The twinkle in her eye didn't go unnoticed either and the shit had my blood boiling. But I had more trying things to worry about.

Will's disappearance is the focus of the team and I had to defuse that shit. One thing I didn't need was muthafuckas breathing down my neck about where he was. At least I didn't have to worry about Stone coming back to retaliate because Rocko handled that issue for sure. All I needed to do was get some work for my team before they started leaving. I'd already lost major members, but that wasn't going to stop what I have planned.

"Are you going to sit in this room all day?" Summer asked from the doorway of my office. "We need to go to the club and handle the inventory, Heat."

"That's what the fuck I pay you for. Since when you need me there to babysit yo' ass?"

"Heat, this is the monthly inventory! We always handle that shit together. If you stop thinking about Kenzie's hoe ass, you would be able to think straight. What is it about her?" Summer screamed. "The bitch said you're in love with her. Is it true?"

I sighed heavily because Summer was asking questions she wasn't ready to hear the answer to. Staring at the wall, I tried my best to ignore her. It was true, I loved Summer, but I was in love with Kenzie's young ass. Her ambition, drive, and determination were unmatched. Kenzie didn't need me, I needed her. Summer, on the other hand, needed me for every fuckin' thing. Hell, without me, she wasn't shit.

"Now you can't hear, nigga?"

"I heard you. I'm not going to entertain you by answering your questions. You are here in my home, Summer. If I didn't love you, believe me, you wouldn't be in this muthafucka. How many times do I have to tell you to concentrate on what we have? Leave all that other shit alone. You gon' stroke out worry about Kenzie."

I stood from my seat and walked toward her. "Another thing, don't let Tiffany get you fucked up. Stay the fuck away from Kenzie and her sister. Fighting out in the streets isn't a good look, especially in and around my establishment. I have other things to worry about. Don't let it happen again. Let's go."

I walked past her ass and grabbed my keys off the island before heading toward the garage. As I sat in the car waiting for Summer to come out, I picked up my phone and hoovered over Kenzie's name. Placing the phone back in the cupholder, I decided I would give her time before I tried contacting her. There was no way I was going to let Kenzie walk out of my life.

At that moment, Summer opened the door and I didn't even notice here come out of the house. The scowl on her face told me she was still on her bitter bullshit. I started the car and backed out of my driveway. The silence inside my whip was better than listening to her bitch and moan about Kenzie. I knew Summer had so much more to say, but she knew better.

When I pulled into the club's parking lot, I got a bad feeling in my gut. Glancing around before I attempted to get out, the lot was empty. We had several hours before any patrons would come through for happy hour. Summer and I got out of the car and I walked quickly to unlock the door. Stepping inside, I hit the light switch and went straight to the back.

It took about an hour to count the inventory and stock the bars. Summer had been glaring at me the whole time. If looks could kill, I'd be a dead man. I didn't know why she was so upset. She knew what the fuck it was before hopping on my joint. It was my fault for fuckin' her and keeping her ass around. She left my ass to finish up, claiming she was tired.

Exiting the stockroom with a case of Hennessy in my hands, the main door opened. Two masked men entered with pistols pointed in my direction. I dropped that shit and took off, but I wasn't fast enough. Bullets started flying around me as I dived for cover. A stinging sensation ran up my leg and I knew I was hit. My stupid ass wasn't strapped so I was like a sitting duck in that muthafucka.

"Bring yo' ass out, nigga! Where the fuck is my money?"

I knew right off the bat who was gunnin' for me. Brando was a young nigga that had a lot of juice in the streets. A few months back, I let him wash his money through the club and he was trying to fuck me over with the payments. Since he wanted to play with me, I took what I thought I was rightfully owed. Instead of coming to me to talk about the change, he came guns blazing and wasn't shit I could do about it.

"You gon' die in this bitch today, Heat! Don't nobody fuck with my money, nigga!"

I could hear footsteps coming in my direction as I used my good leg to push off the floor towards the back door. Cursing myself for leaving my tool in the car, the only thing I could do was pray. God probably wouldn't help my ass because of all the dirt I've done to other muthafuckas, but it was worth a try. The door to my office wasn't too far away, but I didn't think I was going to make it.

Brando appeared and I knew death was my next destination. If I was going to go out, it wouldn't be with me begging for my fuckin' life. "Where's my shit, Heat? You may as well tell me, bitch! You gon' die anyway. Plus, where you going, you won't be able to spend my money. Just tell me where the fuck I can find it!"

"Fuck you, lil nigga!" I laughed. "Kill me and stop talking about what you gon' do! I'm not telling you shit!"

Brando was so worried about the money he had yet to pull the trigga. If he was a real hitta, I wouldn't have still been breathing to talk shit to his ass. Greed overtakes the real problem any day. Luck was on his side because I was the only other person in the club. This muthafucka was going to torture me in order to get his bread.

"You should've compensated me a reasonable commission and I wouldn't have had to take yo' shit! The pennies you tried to come at me with was a no-go, nigga. I didn't agree to any of that shit. But I bet I came out on top when I hit yo' muthafuckin' pockets." Brando didn't like what I said and sent a warning shot to the left of my head.

"Stop fuckin' around and unass my money!" he sneered.

"Why are you playing with this punk, Brando? Kill his ass!" his partner screamed. "You wasting too much time talking to this muthafucka. Fuck it, I'll off him myself!" The unknown nigga lifted his gun and soon as he pulled the trigger, Brando hit his arm upward and the bullet went into the ceiling.

Gunshots came out of nowhere. Brando and his partner in crime hit the floor with bullets riddled in their bodies. Crawling in the direction of my office, I looked back and Rocko turned the corner with a grimace on his face. Relief washed over me as I sprawled on the floor and looked up at the ceiling, thanking the man above for sending help my way. Rocko took his phone from his hip as he made his way to me.

"A pipe busted on the main floor, need it fixed now!" he screamed into the phone before hanging up. "You gon' be good, Heat. Who the fuck is them niggas and why the fuck they coming for you?" he asked, taking a bandana out of his pocket and tying it around my thigh to slow down the bleeding.

I wanted to lie to him and say I didn't know, but I owed him the truth since he saved my life. Hopefully, Rocko didn't judge me for my actions. "That's Brando. I was letting him wash his money through the club and he didn't want to come off the cash; so, I took his shit. I'd been skimmin' off his shit for a couple months. Instead of him coming to talk about the situation, he came shooting first."

"Heat, you would've done the same thing! You lucky I was driving by and decided to come in to chop it up with you. This ain't over. His people coming for you, man. You gon' have to lay low for a while."

"I'm not about to go into hiding for these muthafuckas, Rocko—"

"You don't have a choice, Heat! It's not the time to be stupid. You have to think logically here, fam. We have the shit with Stone and Tornado hanging over our heads. Don't forget about Will too nigga. Shit is too hot to be trying to be a bad azz. There's only a matter of time before Storm start coming around asking questions."

"There's no way they can pin none of that shit on me!" I said massaging my thigh. "Everybody is dead and there's no way I can be questioned about anything, get that shit out ya head. Long as you keep yo' mouth closed, we good, my nigga."

"I'm not saying shit, Heat. You got my word on that." Rocko bent down and draped my arm over his shoulder so I could get up. "Soon as the cleanup crew gets here, I'm taking you to my crib so Doc can get you right. Then you have to leave town for a minute."

Before I could respond, Rocko's cell started going off and I knew the cleanup crew was outside. He placed me in the nearest chair and went to let them in. I leaned to the side and took out my keys and removed the key to the club from the ring. Since I was going away, I wanted Rocko to have access to the club while I was gone. But business would be closed until further notice.

I was pissed about how shit had gone down because money was already coming in slow and now, I had to close up shop because I got caught slipping. When Brando and his side-kick first entered my establishment, I thought Summer had set my ass up like my baby mama had a couple of years prior. She got lucky because she packed up and moved with my son. I hadn't heard from her since. Summer wouldn't have been that lucky though. There was no way I would've let a bitch snake me again.

The cleanup crew came in and got right to work. Rocko came back over to me after giving orders and was ready to get me to Doc. "I hit Doc up and he gon' meet us at my crib," he said, standing over me.

The pain in my leg was excruciating. I was breathing hard as hell, trying not to yelp out in pain. I was hit at least twice, but I was still alive to talk about it. "Aight. I need to go to my office to erase all the footage before I go," I said, handing him the keys. "I need you to come check on the club every so often to make sure shit good while I'm gone. Business is going to halt until I'm well enough to come back and shit blow over.

"I can do that. You need to holla at the rest of the team to tell them what's up, Heat. We can't have muthafuckas out here blind, not knowing what the fuck going on. It's the profes-sional way to do this shit. I'm quite sure Brando knew everybody on your team and his people may try to come for us when they can't get to you. Ya feel me?"

Rocko was right. I'd tell the team members that's been true to me, but fuck the rest of 'em. If something happened to their ass, oh well. My right hand led me to the office and I completed the task in a matter of minutes. As we were leaving, the cleanup crew was gathering their tools, and there wasn't any evidence of anything ever happening, other than the holes in the walls. I'd get that shit fixed before opening the club back up.

Meesha

Chapter 14

Stone

It's been a week since I was discharged from the hospital. With my house no longer standing, I had choices of where I would lay my head. Going to my parents' home was a no-go because regardless of age, there was still a curfew. I wasn't for that shit, I was a grown ass man. It wasn't as if I was a bum ass nigga, I worked hard for the position I was in. Circumstances forced me to live under someone else's roof.

I chose to stay with my sister, Sam, because I would've been in jail had I took Celeste up on her offer. Celeste had been to the house every day and Joe called every five minutes talking shit. Visibly checking her over head to toe, I didn't see any signs of physical abuse, but I knew that nigga was tearing her down internally. The day I fucked him up was coming soon, but until then, I was going to pay close attention.

Thoughts of Angel swam in my head constantly as I laid in bed. Something didn't feel right about her passing. I didn't feel her spiritual presence around me and it only gave me hope that she wasn't really dead. Even though Scony said he couldn't view her remains at the morgue, I needed to see her for myself. My plans were to travel to Chicago when Scony called to say she arrived at the funeral home.

I'd been in and out of the guest room since I had arrived and it gave me too much time to think. Out of nowhere, moans started coming from the other side of the wall. Sam and her bitch were at it again. From the time they got home and into that damn room, those two couldn't keep their mouths off each other. For breakfast, lunch and dinner, that's all the fuck they did. I didn't knock what they had going on, but damn, be considerate of my black ass.

Putting my feet in my kicks, I didn't know how much longer I would be able to deal with the shit. Every night it was like listening to an Ebony lesbian video on *Pornhub*. I grabbed my keys and wallet from the dresser and made my way out the door. When I got to my car, I looked at the scratches on the hood and it brought me back to the dreadful day that would forever bring me pain.

As I pulled out of the driveway, I just drove because I didn't know where I was heading. Getting out of the house was my main objective. Driving in the direction of the mall, I decided to go buy a couple more outfits since I'd lost everything inside my home. Lucky for me, my safe was saved, but it was being held by the fuckin' FBI until their investigation was complete.

All my shit was legit because my contracts were encrypted to appear as if they were for my businesses. That was the least of my worries, my shit was air tight. I found a park and cut the engine and got out. My car was scheduled to get fix the next day and I couldn't wait because I couldn't continue to roll around with my baby looking like she had been in a catfight.

I walked into the mall and when straight to Foot Locker to cop some jays. I hit up a couple more stores and had bags in each hand. Going to the food court, I had to hit up my realtor to find a new crib as soon as possible because I needed my own space. Standing in line, I decided I didn't want fast food so, I headed for the exit so I could hit Buffalo Wild Wings.

It didn't take long for me to be seated. The server was a lil cutie and there was nothing wrong with looking. She looked young as hell but baby girl was stacked. I was out in the streets looking like a trap nigga. Wearing a white t-shirt with Balenciaga across the front, a pair of black jeans that hung low on my waist, with my black Timbs on my feet. My fitted was turned backwards on my head and my goatee was on point.

Shawty led me to an empty booth with a huge smile on her face. Taking my seat, she stood still with the same animated grin on her face. I was all for her giving good customer service but allow a nigga to look over the menu first.

"Give me a minute, lil mama. I don't know what I want yet, but you can bring a glass of Tropicana lemonade and some water, please."

"Okay, I'll bring that right back for you," she winked. Ole girl couldn't be no older than seventeen, eighteen years old. Too young for me, that's for sure. If I put my dick in her life, she would stalk the shit out of my ass and I wasn't for the drama.

I decided to order the 15/15 buffalo wing bundle with fries. The *Houston Astros* baseball game was on the television directly in front of me and they were getting beat by the *Tampa Bay Rays*. I wasn't into baseball but anything was better than sitting alone looking dumb. It also took my mind off all the bullshit that I'd gone through in the past two weeks.

"Here's your drinks," the young waitress sang as she placed the cups on the table. "Are you ready to order?"

"Yeah, I'll take that 15/15 buffalo wing bundle with fries. I would like ranch on the side and some barbeque sauce too."

As she reached over to collect the menu, her right breast brushed against the back of my hand. When she stood, her nipple was erect and I guess that's how baby girl acquired her tips. She didn't have to do all that for me.

"Let me explain something to you, shawty. Stop with all the extra shit and conduct yourself in a professional manner. If you are feeling a nigga, say that shit. You don't have to use your body to get the attention of any man out here. You're beautiful, own that shit and know your worth. Never lower your standards for anybody." The smile disappeared from her face and she looked down at the menu she was holding.

"Hold yo' head up, ma. There's nothing for you to be ashamed about. I'm teaching you something your father, brothers, and uncles should've taught you before you get caught up. You are a beautiful queen and I want you to carry yourself as such. I didn't say all of this to put you down, it's a learning process. Any other nigga would've taken advantage of the advances you threw my way. I'm not that type of man. Don't let my appearance fool you. Keep that in mind."

Nadia was the name displayed on her nametag and she scurried off quickly without uttering a vowel. Somebody needed to tell her the truth, it just so happened to be me. I had sisters and kept my foot in their asses back in the day. But both of them went in their own direction and I would forever be there to keep their heads lifted under any situation.

It took about fifteen minutes for my food to arrive and Nadia wasn't the waitress to deliver it to me. Embarrassing the young girl wasn't my intention. Hopefully, that wasn't how Nadia took what I had said. Digging into my wings, I watched the rest of the baseball game as I ate. Halfway through my meal, my phone started ringing. I caught the call at its last ring after cleaning my hands, I pressed the button quickly.

"What's up?" I asked into the phone, taking a sip of my lemonade.

"Stone, it's Scony. Who else was at yo' crib the day of the incident?" Scony agitatedly asked.

"Nobody. Angel was the only person there after our argument. Why would you ask that?"

"I just got off the phone with the medical examiner, this shit ain't making sense, my nigga. They haven't shipped Nicassy's body because it ain't her lying in the muthafuckin' morgue! The person is male and the examiner wouldn't answer my questions any further because the body's been turned over to the FBI. They will be contacting me soon, but I thought

I would shoot the information to you, because if they gon' contact me, they will be rollin' up on you too."

"I'm confused, what the fuck you mean the body they got is a nigga? How is that?" I asked confused.

"I don't know but soon as they contact me, I will let you know what's going down. Stone, I need you to think about who the fuck could've been in your shit. We need to figure this shit out."

"Scony, I have no clue who it could've been. This shit got me stumped like a muthafucka."

"I gotta find my fuckin' sister and I need yo' ass to think! Get the fuck off my phone, man. Be ready when them people hit you up and you better tell them everything without leaving anything out!"

Scony hung up on me and I lost my appetite. Leaving the rest of my wings on the table along with a hefty tip for Nadia, I walked out of the restaurant. Hearing Scony say Angel's body wasn't found had me thinking about the muthafucka that was actually there. It had been damn near two weeks, if she was alive, she would've reached out to somebody by now.

I hit the key fob to unlock the doors of my whip and jump in. Speeding out of the parking lot, I headed toward Onyx to pick up money and make sure things were running smoothly. My boy JDubb was keeping me posted about everything that was going on, but I wanted to see for myself.

It was seven o'clock and the happy hour folks were in the club getting their early day party on. I hadn't been in my establishment since before the incident at my home. When I stepped in the door, people greeted me with hugs and handshakes. The love I received was everything to me but I wasn't in the partying mood. Making my way to my office, I sat down in the chair behind my desk and watched the venue from the monitor. There was a light knock on the door, then it opened.

"It's good to finally lay eyes on you outside of that damn hospital bed, nigga." JDubb closed the door behind him and crossed the room. I stood up and gave him a brotherly hug. "I didn't know where you were to pull up on you to make sure you were straight. That's why I was sending text messages about every little thing just so you would respond."

"Man, why didn't you just ask," I laughed as I sat down in the chair. "How's everything coming along?" I asked.

"Everything is running smoothly. Your money is in the safe and yes, it's all there. I had to fire Melody because she was in this muthafucka fighting last week," JDubb explained.

"Shid, she had to be out of control if you fired her ass. You were in charge so I have nothing to say about the shit."

I raised up and went straight to the closet where my safe was located. After inspecting the money inside, I bent down to get my duffle bag to carry my cash in. The trap door in the floor caught my attention and I had to do a double take.

"Dubb, were you fuckin' with that hatch in the floor?" I asked, still looking down. The only way anyone would even notice it was if they were searching my shit. I didn't like a nosy muthafucka. Invading my privacy was a no-go when it came to me and my business.

"What hatch is you talking about, Boss?" he asked entering the closet behind me. "Far as I went was the safe. I put in the code, stashed the money, locked that bitch up, and bounced. I didn't know nothing about a door in the floor, my nigga."

"My bad, I must've left it open. I'm trippin'. Is there anything else you need from me? I'm about to head out."

"Nah. I'm going back on the floor to make sure the bartenders ain't overpouring the alcohol. I'm glad you good, man. I can't wait to have you back in here turning up on a Friday night."

"I'll be back soon. Keep doing what you doing, Dubb. I appreciate you and that raise got yo' ass running my shit better than me," I laughed. "Hopefully, the logs match the money."

"Of course, it does. I was taught at a young age not to bite the hand that fed me. You feed a nigga too good to fuck up that cash flow. Come on so I can walk you out to your whip. Knowing yo' ass, you ain't even strapped."

"You a muthafuckin' lie. My bitch is part of me and move when I move, nigga," I said, raising the back of my shirt. I zipped the bag and swung the strap over my shoulder and headed for the door. Dubb locked my office up holding the keys out for me to take. "Nah, hold on to those. I won't be back until I find another house and finish healing. I still get mild headaches out of the blue so I don't want to jump back into things too quickly. We will keep things going this way until further notice, if you're up for the position."

"Hell yeah, I'll hold you down. Take as long as you need, Stone. I got ya back."

Dubb led the way through the club and out of the door. He stood guard until I got the bag into the trunk and I was seated comfortably in the driver's seat. Soon as I turned the key in the ignition, he stepped back and nodded his head at me. I did the same in return and back out of the parking spot.

As I drove through the Houston streets, I ended up outside of my partially burned home. The entire front of the house was destroyed, and the back had holes in the ceiling, but seemed to be intact. My mind went back to the hatch in the floor of my office at Onyx and my heart started beating fast.

Jumping out of my car, I ran to the side gate and to the back of the yard. That entire part of the house only had minor damage. Scony's words echoed in my head. *The body didn't belong to Nicassy. The body didn't belong to Nicassy.*

Meesha

Chapter 15

Phantom

"Xavier, you don't have concrete evidence of Tiffany endangering Layla's life. There isn't anything other than your word to back up your claim. We need more."

The process to getting full custody of Layla was going to be hell and it was already getting on my nerves. I was sitting across from my lawyer Chanel at Thomas &Thomas Law but the shit she was saying didn't sit right with me. Of all people, Chanel knew the type of bitch Tiffany was but now she wanted to go by the fuckin' book.

"What more do you need? The muthafucka that she's with is beating the shit out of her! What proof do I need? I'm not waiting until he decides to hurt my daughter before any type of action is taken!"

"Phantom, stop raising your fuckin' voice at me," Chanel said calmly. "I want you to use your Xavier voice and leave that street shit outside my door. You will get nowhere being belligerent in this type of situation. Have you gotten the police involved after learning this guy was abusing Tiffany?"

Staring at Chanel like she had another head growing out of her neck, all I could do was shake my head. "I don't fuck with twelve," I growl. "The last time that nigga put his hands on her, I shot his ass."

"I'm going to act like I didn't hear what you just said, Xavier. You're gonna have to involve law enforcement to get a paper trail going. At this point, all you have is what the judge would call speculation. Tiffany will come into the courtroom denying all allegations against her. Making you look like the man that's trying to keep her away from her daughter. I know this isn't what you want to hear, but it's the truth. Get me something to work with."

I was pissed because I didn't have anything to prove what Tiff was going through. Getting the fuckin' pigs involved in my life was a sucka move to me and I wasn't with it. Long as I had my daughter with me, nothing was going to happen to her. As for her mammy, that bitch could keep getting knocked upside her head, I didn't give a fuck.

"It's not what I wanted to hear, but it is what it is. Layla is with me and she's not going back to that house until that nigga is gone." I sat back in the chair and folded my arms over my chest.

"Did Tiffany agree to those terms, Xavier?"

"The bitch don't have a choice! My daughter's life will not be put in jeopardy because of the stupid decisions she wants to make. It's not happening."

"All Tiffany has to do is send the police to your house and you're going to have to allow Layla to go with her mom. You don't have a court order to keep her away from the child you guys have together, Xavier. That's not how you do things." Chanel was getting frustrated and it showed on her face. "There's nothing more I can do for you, honestly. Start keeping documentation of events and get the police involved. After that, we will have something to go on. Until then, my hands are tied."

"That's bullshit, Chanel! You know what type of woman Tiffany is!" I sneered.

"I know enough as the woman you were sleeping with, Xavier. All of her animosity was towards you and I because we were together. What's going on now, I don't know shit about, so don't pan me out to be a fuckin' liar." The professionalism was gone from Chanel's voice and I knew I'd pushed her too far.

"How about we go grab something to eat so we can talk freely outside of your job?"

"Yeah, that sounds good to me." Chanel turned off her computer and locked her files in the desk drawer. She grabbed her purse and we both stood at the same time. "You have your nerve coming at me in that manner," she said, rolling her eyes as she stormed toward the door.

"Fuck! Phantom, damn this dick still feels amazing."

Chanel and I didn't end up going out for lunch. Instead, I had her head down ass up at the *Marriott* hotel a couple blocks from her office. She was clutching the sheets for dear life as I caressed her folds. With every stroke, her ass rippled like a tidal wave and the shit looked and felt good. My balls were tingling and my toes curled tightly as I fought to hold my nut. When she clenched her walls, it was game over for me.

"Shit, Chanel," I growled as I emptied my kids into the condom that covered my pipe. Smacking her repeatedly on her ass, she threw it back, milking me for every drop of my semen.

As my joint slid from her love box, Chanel laid spread eagle on the bed. Her secretions leaked out of her pussy and my mouth watered instantaneously but I shook the thought of licking her from ass to appetite from my head. Climbing out of the bed, I went into the bathroom and flushed the condom before stepping in the shower.

The water cascaded over my head and Kenzie's face appeared behind my eyelids. Guilt tried to enter my soul but I wasn't allowing it. Kenzie wasn't trying to be with me, no matter how hard I'd tried to convince her. A nigga had needs that hadn't been met, I needed some pussy.

Kenzie hadn't answered any of my calls since the day her brother came to Atlanta. I consoled her until she fell asleep then left and went to pick up Layla from my mom. I've called to check on her with no response. It bothered me, but I let her have that shit.

"Can I join you?" Chanel's voice brought me back to reality as she stepped into the shower before I could respond. I took that opportunity to grab the towel I had in my hand and lathered it with soap. Washing quickly, I got out and still hadn't said anything to her. Chanel was staring a hole in my back but I wasn't about to play any games with her.

"So, that's it, Xavier?"

"Look, Chanel. You knew what the fuck this was when you agreed to come here with me. We tried the relationship thing and it didn't work. I thought we were both adults, man. Don't let this shit fuck up the business we have together. We fucked and that's all it was for both of us."

"Nawl, that's all it was for you! There must be someone in your life that has your heart in the palm of her hand. All the other hoes you fuck with has never had you acting like this." Chanel had a whole attitude with me.

"It's something like that, but you know how things are with us, Chanel. You are a damn good lawyer, but you are not the woman for me. It was my mama's idea for me to contact you to take my case. I could've found someone else but I trust you to handle business for me. If you can't put your feelings aside and help me with this, let me know now."

"It's cool. I'm going to act like this didn't happen. Believe me, it won't happen again," she said, slamming the shower door closed.

Drying off with one of the towels, I entered the room and started putting my clothes on. Chanel walked in with all of her glory out for me to see, but it did nothing for me. Once I was dressed, I walked across the room and sat in a chair gazing out the window. The sound of the door opening caused me to look up. Chanel walking out of the room with her head held high was all I saw as the door closed behind her.

***

As I pulled up to my mama's house, there were two squad cars and a belligerent Tiffany screaming and hollering in my OG's face. I jumped out of my whip and stormed up the walkway. An officer tried to stop me but I pulled out of his grasp and continued toward my mama.

"Bring my daughter out here now, Karla!" Tiffany screamed.

"Disrespect my mama one more time and I'll be going to jail for fuckin' you up!" Tiffany's eyes got big as saucers when she saw me climb the stairs and stand next to my mother. "I told you what you had to do in order to take my daughter away from me. Have you done it yet?"

"Fuck you, Xavier! I'm leaving here with my daughter today. These police officers ain't here because your mama called them. I brought them to escort me over here." She grinned.

"I don't give a damn who you brought with you. Layla isn't going anywhere with you. The environment you live in is not suitable for *my* daughter."

One of the officer's step between Tiffany and the stairs and put his hands out. "That's enough! From this point on, I will be the only person asking the questions. Mr.—"

"Bennett," I said, giving my last name.

"Mr. Bennett, do you have court documentation stating Ms. Flowers can't take the child off the premises?"

"No, but—"

"Enough said," the officer cut me off before I could complete what I was about to say. "Go inside and get the child, Mr. Bennett."

"I'm not going to get shit! My daughter is not leaving this house with her! I'd be damned if the nigga that's whoopin' her ass gets the chance to put his hands on my daughter! Get the fuck outta here!"

I was mad as hell because the fuckin' police were putting my daughter in jeopardy by trying to tear her away from me and back into the arms of her trifling ass mama. The bitch was doing all this shit out of spite and she knew the bullshit was going to hurt a muthafucka. I wanted to grab her ass by the neck and squeeze the life out of her funky ass.

"Xavier, it's not worth you going to jail over this. I'm going inside to get Layla," my mama said as she rubbed my back. "It's going to be alright, son."

My whole body was burning like hot coal I was so mad. I watched my mama enter the house and tears formed in my eyes. Layla was everything to me and being in her mama's custody wasn't where she belonged.

"Mr. Bennett, if you feel the child belongs with you, my only advice is to fight for custody. Until you do that, you can't withhold the child from her mother when technically she has sole custody."

The officer tried to explain but that shit went in one ear and out the other. Layla stepped out of the house and threw her arms around my waist. Prying her loose was a task but I manage to get it done. I got down eye level with my daughter and wiped the tears from her face.

"I don't want to go, Daddy. Please don't make me go," Layla wailed.

"There's nothing I can do, baby. I promise, I'm gon' fight for you, Layla. Be strong for me, baby. I'm coming for you. I don't care what time or day, if you need me; call me. Where's your phone?" Layla took her phone from her bag and handed it to me. I programmed Kenzie's number in it and put it back in her bag. "You have your granny, Uncle Kannon, Auntie Kimille, and Kenzie's number in there, okay?"

"Okay, Daddy. I love you."

"I love you too, Lay. Remember, I'm coming for you," I said hugging her tight. Releasing her, I kissed her forehead and stood to my feet.

Watching my baby walk slowly down the steps, she looked back at me with the saddest eyes and I fought hard not to cry. As I watched Tiff lead my daughter away from me, I shook my head and held my bottom lip between my teeth until I tasted blood. Tiff sat behind the wheel of her car with a smile on her face. Soon as the police moved their vehicles so she could leave, she waved and blew a kiss at me.

I watched the car until it was out of sight. If anything happened to my daughter, that bitch was good as dead. My mama hugged me from behind and I broke. Everyone knew my daughter was the beat to my heart. Without her I was nothing. My body was shaking and I needed to calm down before I hopped in my whip to beat that bitch ass.

"Xavier, it's going to be alright. Did you contact Chanel like I suggested?"

"I met up with her before coming here, she jinxed me! Chanel said all Tiff had to do was call the police to escort her to pick up Layla and that's exactly what her ugly ass did!" I screamed as I shrugged my mama off and started pacing back and forth.

"What happens now?" she asked.

"Chanel basically told me exactly what the cop said. I need to have proof that Layla is in danger and I don't have none of that. Documentation is a must before I can even attempt to take it to court. In other words, there's nothing I can do unless something happens to my baby!" I cried. "By then, it will be too late to contact anybody, because I'm killing every fuckin' body on sight!"

"We're going to keep a positive mind. Nothing's going to happen to her, Xavier. Come inside and rest your mind. I don't want you out and about right now. The last thing I need you to do is drive to that girl's house."

"I'm not thinking about her, but I'll stay for a little bit just for you."

Me and my mama sat watching TV until I dozed off on her couch. Not realizing how exhausted I was, I ended up staying the night. Being in the comfort of my mother's home, brought a slight sense of peace.

Chapter 16

Loco

Mya was riding the fuck out of my joint. When my phone started ringing, "Nigga, you bet not even think about reaching for that shit!" Mya moaned as she rolled her ass in a circular motion. My eyes rolled to the back of my head, causing me to grip her waist tightly.

"Shit! Ride this dick, bitch!"

Thrusting my hips repeatedly upward, Mya was bouncing wildly from the way my shit was attacking her vaginal canal. I grabbed both breasts and rolled the nipples between my fingers. Mya splashed all her juices on me and it was warm and gushy, just how I liked it. The tightness of her walls sucked the nut out of me prematurely.

"Aaaah fuck… shit, girl!" I screamed out, louder than intended.

Slowly easing in and out of Mya's honey pot, my phone started ringing again. I couldn't ignore it, so I rolled over causing Mya to topple over. She kicked me in the shin as she smacked her lips.

"Next time you want some pussy, find it somewhere else since your phone is more important than mine," she huffed.

"Shut the fuck up, this business!" I yelled, seeing Heat's name on my screen as I answered. "What's up, Boss?"

"Stay low. Some shit went down at the club and I had to get ghost. Brando's crew may be out for blood after this one, watch yo' back." Heat was talking in such a rushed tone, I barely caught what he said.

"Hold up, Heat. Slow down and give me a little bit more to go off of. What the fuck is going on?" I asked, sitting up.

"That's all I can say over the phone. Keep your eyes open for Brando's crew. I gotta go."

Heat hung up without saying much of anything else. If I was in danger behind his ass, he should've told me exactly what the fuck I was up against. Brando wasn't shit to play with and this nigga gave me a watered down version of nothing. It wasn't that I couldn't hold my own against him and his crew, hell, I needed to know what was up.

"What was that about?" Mya asked, coming back into the room. She had left after catching an attitude when I answered my phone.

"I don't know. Heat said something about watching out for Brando's crew—"

"Oh my God! Brando was killed the other day. His body was found in Freedom Park, along with one of his workers. Word on the street is, it was a robbery gone bad, but his crew ain't buying the story and is offering a hunnid bands for information. Did Heat off that nigga, Loco?"

Mya had a terrifying look in her eyes as she stared at me. I hadn't heard anything about the shooting because I hadn't really been out of the crib. Mya stayed her ass outside and knew a hell of a lot about the incident. I needed to know everything she'd heard so I would have an understanding of what I was dealing with.

"I don't know if Heat did it or not. How do you know so much about what happened?" I asked curiously.

"One of my girls fucks with one of Brando's people. She was talking about it when we went out for drinks the other night. Thinking back on the conversation, she was looking at me funny, as if she was studying my reaction. I could be just paranoid because Heat mentioned Brando's name to you."

"Well, if the bitch reaches out again, don't say shit about nothing! Do she know anything about you? Where you lay your head? That I'm yo' nigga?" I asked, trying to see how much this bitch knew about me.

"Of course, she knows, she's my friend. You know Alicia. She's been over here before, Loco. But you don't have to worry about her. She's solid. Enough about this shit, you fucked me so good I'm hungry. Let's go out and get something to eat."

Going out was the last thing I wanted to do, but not going out would make muthafuckas think I was in hiding. Shit, I didn't pull the muthafuckin' trigger, so I had nothing to worry about. I wanted to order something and have it delivered, but Mya was already getting dressed to go out. Standing to my feet, I went to take a leak and a quick shower. Thoughts of how Heat rolled out without hollering at us in person, rubbed me the wrong way.

After getting dressed, I threw on a pair of joggers, a t-shirt, and slid my feet in my sneakers before grabbing my keys off the dresser. "What do you have a taste for?" I asked Mya as I walked past and smacked her on the ass.

"I want seafood. Let's go to *Pappadeaux's*."

That was right up my alley. You could never go wrong when it came to seafood. I couldn't understand how some folks could say crab and lobster was nasty. That shit hit like good pussy in my book. Leading the way through the house, I opened the door so Mya could walk out first, then I stepped out to lock the door. My girl gasped and the hairs on the back of my neck stood up like a scared feline.

"Open the muthafuckin' door and get back inside!" Turning to look over my shoulder, I was hit on the side of the head with a hard object. "Don't fuckin' look at me, nigga! Open the fuckin' door!"

Doing as I was told, I twisted the doorknob and walked back into my house. The nigga behind me pushed Mya onto the floor and I did an about face when I saw her fall to her knees. Raising my fist to knock his head off his shoulders, I paused because the nigga had his Glock smiling in my face.

"What you gon' do, nigga? Hit me?" He laughed. "Take yo' best shot, muthafucka!"

"Put the fuckin' gun down! I'm at a disadvantage. If I hit you, yo' ass gon' pull the trigga. Fight me heads up!" I snarled.

"I'm not here to fight you, Loco. Yo' boss took mine from me, and I want to know where his muthafuckin' ass is!"

"Who the fuck is yo' boss? I don't even know what the fuck you talking about, nigga. Whatever the fuck you think Heat did ain't got shit to do with me. Go take that shit up with his ass! I don't know where he is, go find him! Get the fuck outta my face," I said, standing tall as I looked this nigga in his face.

The dude standing before me is somebody I didn't know from a can of paint. He came bombarding his way into my house with a pistol, pushing my girl to the floor, and raising his muthafuckin' voice like that shit was going to scare me. Mya started crawling slowly toward the couch and I knew she was going for the tool that I kept under there. I prayed the whole time I watched her out the corner of my eye.

"Bitch, where the fuck you going?" he shouted, pulling a second gun from his waist and pointed it at Mya. She paused and laid her head onto the carpet with her arms stretched wide. "Move again and I will blow yo' shit back!"

"Keep that shit over here, nigga. She ain't got nothing to do with this bullshit! Hell, I don't have a damn thing to do with it but here we are! Who the fuck are you?" I asked.

"It don't matter! Where the fuck is Heat? You got to the count of five to tell me what I want to know."

I was going to call his bluff. This muthafucka wasn't gon' do shit. His hands were slightly shaking and I knew he was nervous. Whoever sent him to do a grown man's job, failed miserably. He took his eyes off me for a split second. I lunged at him and a shot rang out, halting my movements. Looking over my shoulder, Mya had a bullet in the back of her head and blood was spilling out fast.

"Mya!" I screamed, rushing to her side. She didn't move and her eyes were wide open. The sight before me broke my heart.

Mya was the love of my life and there was no way I could go on without her. Watching as she took her last breath killed me and I knew this nigga wasn't going to walk out of my house with me still being alive. Diving for the pistol under the couch, he pulled the trigger and I felt the hot lead in the small of my back. I lost all feeling in my lower body and I couldn't move another inch. Kicking me in my side, I was rolled unto my back and stared up into the barrel of the gun.

"Where is Heat?"

"Fuck you! Kill me, muthafucka, because I'm not telling you shit!"

"Aight," was all he said before he sent a bullet into my forehead. Mya ran into my arms as she smiled. I knew we were going to live eternally together for the rest of our lives.

Meesha

Chapter 17

Dreux

I had been searching high and low for Heat, but he was nowhere to be found. Nobody from the team was answering any of my calls and that shit was unusual. It was strange that it happened soon as we found out Tornado had been killed in Houston and Heat's name was involved somehow. When I went to Heat's house, I didn't get an answer. The club was closed and there was a sign on the door indicating it would be that way until further notice. Shit didn't make sense at all.

Contacting Rocko was a dead end too because that nigga wasn't at his home either. I was on my way to Loco's crib because he was my last resort. All of these muthafuckas were on sneaky shit and I didn't like it at all. As I rounded the corner of Loco's block, it seemed as if the whole police force was lining the street. It didn't take a rocket scientist to know something bad happened at his crib.

I wasn't able to drive down the street so I backed out and parked on the next block and walked back over. There was a crowd of people standing around and I blended in. A lot of low chattering was going on and I just stood listening to whatever I could pick up on.

"The nigga that lives here and his girl was murked. This shit got the Black Kings written all over it," one dude said lowly to another.

"How you figure they had something to do with this?"

"Brando was killed the other day. The muthafucka that's laid out cold in there is part of Heat's crew. Heat is the one that offed Brando and they came back to find that nigga because he's missing in action. Them niggas in the Black Kings gang gon' come for all that's associated with Heat. This shit is bad for all involved because the bloodshed is not going to stop here."

"That was my girl Mya in there! She didn't deserve that shit! Loco is a bitch ass nigga and probably knew what the fuck was going on. Now my friend is dead because of him!"

I had heard enough and backed up to walk away as the coroner was wheeling out the two bodies on stretchers. Making my way back to my car, I pulled out my phone and hit up Phantom. I put my whip in drive and pulled out of the parking spot.

"What up, Dreux?"

"Aye, where you at? I need to rap with you ASAP," I said into the phone.

"I'm at the crib. You good?"

"Shit is fucked up. I'll be there in twenty to fill you in."

"Cool, I'm here."

"Bet." Ending the call, I hit the highway and sped all the way to Phantom's crib.

Heat out in the street murdering people without giving a heads up to anybody was a bitch move. He just put all our lives in danger and left, saving his own life. Loco wasn't somebody I was worried about because his days were number on this earth anyway. His mouth was going to get him killed one day, it just so happened to come sooner than expected, and all by the hands of the man he stood ten toes down for.

Arriving at Phantom's crib, I parked my car beside his. I walked up the steps and the door swung opened before I could attempt to ring the doorbell. Phantom stepped to the side and allowed me to enter his home. He led the way to the patio, where he had blunts already rolled and ready.

"What brings you by, big homie?" Phantom asked, flaming up.

148

"I went by Loco's crib to pick his brain on what's been going on with Heat. When I got over there, police were everywhere. Somebody offed him and his bitch today. I stood watching shit unfold as the police went in and out, I overheard some people talking about what they think happened."

"Loco is dead?" Phantom's eyes bulged out of his head as smoke poured from his mouth.

"Yeah. Did you know anything about Heat being into it with Brando from the Black Kings gang?"

"Nawl. Why would Heat have beef with them niggas? We don't fuck around with that drug shit."

Phantom said exactly what I was thinking and that made this shit so much more confusing. The Black Kings moved weight by the boatload and it didn't make sense as to why heat would be involved with any of that shit. We got paid hundreds of thousands off one hit and didn't have to stand on the corner to risk our freedom doing it.

"I'm trying to figure that out myself. Word on the street is, Brando was found dead the other day, and Heat supposedly did it." I stopped talking because things started coming together in my mind. "Thinking back on it, I'd been looking for this nigga Heat all day and he's nowhere to be found. The club is shut down until further notice too. Heat wasn't at his crib and Rocko ain't answering his phone either. Maybe he did have something to do with that shit."

"Hold up! Heat closed down the club?" Phantom asked sitting up in the chair he was leaned back in. "He ain't never did that shit, because he always said there's money to be made and if the club is closed, he couldn't make a dime."

"My point exactly. I also heard while out there that the Black Kings are coming for anybody associated with Heat. With Loco found dead, there's some truth to what was said. We have to warn Kenzie and Kayla. They need to stay out of the way until we can find this nigga Heat. I had intentions to head over to Will's crib and talk to Symone, but after what I learned, I knew I needed to come holla at you."

"I'm gon' hit Kenzie up and tell her and Kayla to stay inside until we can get to them," Phantom said, pulling his phone from his pocket. Kenzie must've not answered because he hit a button again and got the same result. "We can roll over to Will's and I'll keep trying to get hold of Kenzie on the way. I'll call Khaos when we get in the car so he can meet us there. Oh, you driving, nigga. I'm about to burn this spiff and chill in the passenger seat for a change."

Phantom got up, grabbed a couple of blunts and headed inside. I followed behind him as he gathered whatever he was bringing along with him. After locking up, Phantom went to the passenger seat of his car and hurried to mine as he tucked his hammer in the back of his pants. Instead of calling Khaos, Phantom shot him a text. The whole time I drove, his ass huffed and puffed because Kenzie still wasn't answering her phone.

He made another call and put it on speaker. "Yo, fam, call Kayla and tell her and that stubborn ass sister of hers to stay the fuck in the house. Kenzie's not answering for me and I don't need them out and about right now."

"Damn, Cuz, what the fuck goin' on?" Khaos asked.

"I'll fill you in when I see you. Just do that for me and get to Will's crib, me and Dreux almost there."

"Aight. I'm about to do it now."

I concentrated on the road as Phantom seethed because Kenzie still hadn't answered his calls. As I turned down Will's street, there was a glimmer of hope that he was inside when I spotted his truck parked in the driveway. Parking on the street, I waited for Phantom to make the first move to get out before I followed suit. Both of us walked slowly up to the porch when the sounds of *Rick Ross* blared loudly through the streets. Khaos always made his presence known with his damn sounds beating like he was at a rap concert.

"This muthafucka," Phantom mumbled as we watched Khaos hike his pants up as he walked in our directions. "Did you get Kayla on the horn?"

"Nah. What the fuck is going on?" Khaos asked. "Oh, Will finally showed up, I see."

"We about to find out in a minute. Los and his bitch were found murdered earlier, Heat is missing in action, and Rocko ain't answering. The club is closed down and word on the street is Heat murked Brando, the leader of The Black Kings." Phantom summed everything up to his cousin perfectly and hearing that shit had the wheels turning in my head.

"This nigga been moving foul and on top of that, ain't had the decency to warn no damn body. Why are we trying to get in touch with the twins so hard?"

"Those niggas are coming for the whole team until they get to Heat. I want to make sure they're alright."

"Let's get this shit over with so we can go out and look for their asses," Phantom said, jogging up the stairs and pressed the bell.

Waiting for someone to answer the door, Phantom kept ringing the doorbell then started beating on the door like he was the police. After a while, Symone finally opened, looking like she had been through hell and high waters. Her hair was all over her head, she had on a night gown that appeared as if she'd had it on for weeks on end. The dark circles under her eyes let me know she hadn't been sleeping very well.

"Hello, Dreux. Please tell me you've heard from Will." Symone's eyes sparkled with hope. I was hoping she would tell us he was in the house sleep or some shit.

"We were hoping you heard from him," I said sadly. "Can we come in?" Symone stepped back and allowed us to enter her home. "Where's the kids?" I asked as she led the way to the dining room. She sat down in a chair before answering.

"They're with my mother. This shit with Will has taken a toll on me mentally. Will has never went away without calling to check on me and the kids. Somethings not right, Dreux." A lone tear fell from her eye and she quickly wiped it away.

"When was the last time you spoke with him?" Phantom asked crossing his arms over his chest.

"It's been weeks since Will said he had to travel to Houston for business. I haven't heard from him since. He never told me what type of business and I didn't ask. I never wanted to know too much about his line of work."

The words Symone spoke had all three of us looking at one another as the light bulb went off in our heads at the same time. Will never left Houston and it wasn't a coincidence that Nicassy died in the very city he had traveled in the same timeframe.

"Symone, we are trying to track down Will. When I get a lead on his whereabouts, I'll hit you up personally," I said, giving her my word. Symone wiped the tears from her eyes as she followed us to the door.

"Heat stopped by and brought me five hundred thousand dollars—cash. He didn't say what it was for, but no amount of money will make me feel any better not knowing where my husband is. Dreux, I don't care; dead or alive, I want him back here with me. I've already readied myself to accept whatever may have happened. Will is no longer on this cruel earth, please don't be afraid to deliver the news of what I already know. It's been too long for it to be a happy outcome."

I couldn't find any words to give Symone any hope because deep down, I knew my nigga was partying in heaven too. Leaving Will's home, the dots were connected and Heat's involvement was confirmed. Like myself, Will loved those girls. I truly believed Will was killed because he didn't carry out the hit Nicassy botched.

"Hit Kenzie up, Phan! We are all in danger. Even though we walked away from the operation, those niggas in the Black Kings gang don't know shit about that. If they got to Loco, they can definitely go after the twins as easy targets." Phantom pulled his phone out to try once again to get in touch with the twins and I was glad when the line connected.

Putting the phone on speaker, "Hey, I need to talk to you. What's your location?" Phantom asked before Kenzie could say hello.

"Phantom, I'm not in the mood for this right now."

"What's your fuckin' location, Kenzie!" The line was silent for a few seconds before Kenzie sighed loudly into the phone.

"Kayla and I are pulling up to Club Heat. We wanted to inquire about Will."

"Kenzie, listen to me. Keep driving, it's not safe."

"Oh shit!"

A rapid stream of gunfire could be heard on the other end of the phone. Kenzie and Kayla's screams caused my heart to stop beating for a second. Without much thought, we all jumped in our vehicles and hauled ass toward the club.

Meesha

Chapter 18

Kenzie

Phantom had been blowing my phone up, but I didn't feel like talking to him. Fighting the temptations of fuckin' him again was getting hard, but I had to stand my ground. Phantom wanted more than I could offer him, and I wasn't one to play with anyone's emotions. So, the best thing for me to do was keep it all about business. Since we didn't have that in common anymore, what was I talking to him for?

Kayla was driving towards our destination when my phone rang for the umpteenth time. Rolling my eyes, I decided to answer so Phantom could stop calling. Before I could say hello, his voice bellowed through the phone.

"Hey, I need to talk to you. What's your location?" Phantom asked.

Telling him I wasn't in the mood to talk wasn't something he wanted to hear. Phantom demanded to know my location and I hesitated before telling him. I took it a step further and shot my location to his phone. He yelled for us not to stop and to keep driving. Kayla was turning into the parking lot when bullets started flying. We both screamed as we ducked and prayed while Kayla whipped the wheel blindly onto the street trying to get away.

Fumbling in my purse, I pulled out my bitch as the back windshield exploded. "What the fuck!" Kayla screeched.

"Turn right!" I yelled as I glanced behind me to see if we were in the clear.

My sister was driving the fuck out of her Benz like she was part of the cast in the *Fast and Furious*. As she made the right turn, a black Cutlass whipped around the corner behind us, damn near side swiping another vehicle. Checking my clip,

I hurriedly unfastened my seatbelt and turned, firing out the rear window at the car behind us. They were swerving to avoid my slugs but I was aiming for the center, there was no escaping what I sent their way.

From what I could see, there were two people in the car. The passenger leaned out of the window positioning himself on the ledge. I took the opportunity to use his ass as target practice as I lit him up. Pulling the trigger continuously, I hit my target spot on and he fell from the car headfirst onto the pavement. The driver sped up, ramming the back of Kayla's car, forcing us into oncoming traffic.

"Where the fuck are the pigs when we need 'em!" Kayla screamed as she swerved back into the right side of the street.

"Fat muthafuckas in the Dunkin Donuts parking lot! Drive this bitch and get us outta here!" I said, inserting another magazine into my nine.

Kayla's phone rang and she hurriedly connected the phone by pressing the button on the steering wheel. "Khaos, muthafuckas shooting at us! They on our ass," she screamed as she kept her eyes on the road.

She pressed on the gas and pushed her whip to top speed. Out of nowhere, Dreux's car pulled on the left of the Cutlass and Khaos' on the right. The driver didn't stand a chance as they let their tools sing from both sides. I wanted on the action so, I fired into the already broken windshield, fuckin' his body up. Kayla bent the corner and I heard a loud explosion.

Searching around for my phone, I finally spotted it on the floor of the car. Immediately pressing on one of the many missed calls from Phantom, I prayed silently while waiting. When he answered I let out the air I was holding in my lungs.

"Go straight to my crib, we gon' meet y'all there. Kenzie, don't go nowhere else—to my house, now!"

Phantom didn't have to worry about me defying him. After what I had just went through, that shit scared the fuck out of me. I'd been in my share of shootouts but this one was different. That was a muthafuckin' hit!

***

"Bitch, what the fuck just happened?" Kayla asked as we sat in Phantom's driveway.

"I don't know, sis. I've never laid eyes on either of those niggas. Phantom knows something because he warned us not to stop at the club. If they were smart, they would've waited until we parked. Luck was on our sides because we would've been gone had we stopped." Chewing on my stiletto nail, I was nervous as hell. "We will find out when they pull up," I said glancing at the side mirror and I noticed both cars coming to a stop behind us.

Opening the door, I grabbed my purse and stepped out, adjusting my pants over my waist. Kayla's car was fucked up and I could tell she was sad because it showed on her face as she inspected her shit when she got out. Phantom, Dreux, and Khaos stomped toward us looking like demonic triplets. All three of them wore the same murderous expression. Phantom's nostrils flared like a raging bull.

"When I call you like I did today, that means something is wrong! Y'all could've died out there and you let your pride get in the way of answering the fuckin' phone!" I didn't even have anything slick to say back to what he said because he was right. Had I answered when he first called, we wouldn't have even been in the vicinity of the club.

"Let's take this shit inside, Phan. We don't need your nosy ass neighbors knowing our business," Dreux said, stopping

Phantom from going further. He led the way inside his house without saying another word.

I walked straight to the bathroom because the bowel movement that almost made its presence in the seat of my pants through that bullshit was forcing its way out. Fifteen minutes later I was still sitting on the throne when Phantom barged his tough ass in without knocking. His hand went straight to his nose and it served his ass right for invading my privacy.

"Damn, it smelled like something crawled inside you and died! Hurry the fuck up so you can hear what's going on." Slamming the door behind him, I chuckled as I pulled some tissue off the roll.

After cleaning myself, I got out of my clothes and hopped in the shower after what I had done. Wasn't no way I could go back out without washing my ass first. The water felt good and loosened the tension in my whole body. I hurried up and washed and got out as I dried off and got dressed. When I entered the living room, it was empty. Walking slowly around Phantom's home, I heard voices coming from the basement and made my way down the stairs.

Stepping off the last step, Kayla and Khaos was sitting on the loveseat while Phantom and Dreux was posted up at the bar. I silently moved around Phantom and poured a hefty glass of Rémy. I'd prefer tequila but I didn't see any, so anything was better than nothing.

"Y'all want to tell us what that shit was about?" I asked, taking a sip from the glass.

Phantom mugged me before he opened his mouth to give his version of what happened. "Heat's muthafuckin' ass did some dirty shit and didn't feel the need to say shit. He killed a nigga named Brando and his crew is out for blood. They hit

Loco and his bitch Mya earlier today and I guess they caught you and Kayla while he was waiting for Heat to slip up."

"Loco dead?" I asked, not really giving a fuck.

"Yeah, I went to holla at him about Will, but when I got there, cops were everywhere. That was when I found out about the Black Kings, their retaliation, and the fact Heat was suspected of pulling the trigga. I agree with Phantom, this isn't the time not to answer yo' phone. Shit is hot and not just out in the streets. We went to Will's crib and Symone said he went to Houston on business. Will is dead. Ain't no other way to look at the situation. Heat did that shit and now we need to find out who went with Will to Houston. There's missing pieces to this story, we need to find them."

"So, Heat got us in beef we know nothing about?" I asked with an attitude. "We don't have to look for the missing pieces, go find that snake ass nigga Rocko. He is the missing link to this shit. His shifty ass is the guinea pig for Heat's pussy ass."

Digging in my purse, I retrieved my phone and went directly to Heat's contact. Without pressing the call button, I dropped my phone back in its rightful place. Knowing Will died at the hands of someone he trusted pissed me off. For Heat to run off like a bitch put the icing on the cake. He could run but he definitely wouldn't be able to hide. I knew just how we were going to find his ass.

"The way to find Heat is through his bitch. Summer is the one that will lead us right to his hideout."

"Kenzie, if he is gon' I'm quite sure he took Summer with him," Kayla said from across the room.

"I'd bet big money he didn't take that bitch with him. He still got Storm on his brain. Deep down, he's waiting for the right time to reach out to me. He won't be able to invite me wherever he is if Summer is present. Mark my words."

Phantom got up and stormed up the stairs. I didn't give a damn because I was going to do whatever I needed to do in order to get back at Heat's ass. The muthafucka put my life in jeopardy and I wasn't about to let him get away with it. Not to mention, my family was standing in line waiting to get into the pearly gates of heaven behind his bullshit.

"Kenzie, you dodged a bullet today when y'all went behind our backs. You may not make it out next time. Don't do nothing stupid without telling anybody first," Dreux said, going up the stairs behind Phantom.

A couple minutes passed before I got up and went to find Phantom, leaving Kayla and Khaos in the basement. Pushing his bedroom door open, he was laid back on his bed with his eyes closed. Stress was displayed on his face and I knew he was mad at me. I kicked off my shoes and climbed on his King-sized bed and rested my head on the pillow next to him.

Phantom didn't move and never opened his eyes to acknowledge my presence. So, instead of waiting, I took it upon myself to break the ice. "Look, I'm sorry I didn't answer your calls. You know how I feel about the situation we are in."

"Nah, that's all on you, shawty. You can keep playing kiddie ass games and you gon' end up getting hurt out there. Kenzie, you need to listen to what's being said to you. This shit is real and if anything happens to you, I'm gon' die trying to paint this muthafuckin' state red. You don't ever have to be with me, but I will protect you to the best of my ability."

Phantom rolled over and sat on the other side of the bed with his back facing me. He reached in the drawer and pulled out a bag of weed. Phantom's shoulders slumped lowly letting me know there was more to his attitude. He appeared as if the world was weighing down on his shoulders. Once he finished rolling his blunt and set fire to it, I watched him inhale heavily before scooting over to rub his back.

"What's else is going on, Phantom?" I asked softly. Waiting patiently while he smoked half of his blunt, I continued to run my hand up and down his back.

"I was forced by the pigs to give Layla back to Tiff. The shit is bothering me because my baby girl isn't safe there. Hearing the gunshots when I was on the phone with you only heightened my stress level."

"You have to go to the courts and fight for custody. Your stupid ass baby mama isn't fit to have Layla in that house with her," I said sitting up on the bed. "Did you tell the police what's going on in Tiffany's life right now?"

"Without proof there's nothing I can do. It's her word against mine. I'm prepared to fight until I have my daughter back in this house with me. Even my lawyer said I would have to allow Tiff to have Layla if she came to get her, and that's exactly what she did. The only thing I can do is pray nothing happens while she's there, because I'm ready to get sized for an inmate outfit."

Kayla knocked softly on the door and both of us turned our heads. "Hey, sis. Khaos called a tow truck to have my car hauled to the shop. He's about to take me home, you ready?"

"Roll out. Kenzie ain't going no damn where." I guess his word was law because my sister left the doorway with a smirk on her face. I maneuvered my way off the bed and stuffed my feet in my shoes. "Don't get fucked up. Lay yo' ass back down."

Phantom stared at me and I did what I was told and sat my ass back on his bed. I hoped he didn't think we were fuckin' because that shit wasn't even happening. But the way he bossed up did make my yoni tingle a little bit.

Meesha

Chapter 19

Scony

"Malikhi, if you don't stop jumping your little tail around, we're going to have a problem!"

Jade could be heard all the way in my mancave and I sat back to see if my son was going to do as he was told. It was her damn fault he thought everything was a joke because she was always playing with his little ass. "Malikhi, sit down before I get my belt!"

"No, no, no," he laughed loudly as his little feet pattered over my head.

Standing to my feet, I walked slowly up the stairs and peeked out of the door. Malikhi was running around the living room with Jade right behind him. The shit I was witnessing was funny but I dared not to laugh. When Jade got her hands on Malikhi, he was going to wish he had listened. But the way he was giving her a run for her money, she wasn't going to catch him anytime soon. Opening the door, I stepped out and walked to the entryway of the living room and stood there for a few more minutes.

"Khi, come here," I said without raising my voice. My son stopped in his tracks and looked at me then his mom. "I said, come here." My voice boomed a little bit but I still didn't yell. Slowly making his way over where I was standing, Malikhi fumbled with his little fingers with his head held low.

"Hold your head up. Why do you have to be told twice to do something?" I asked as I leaned against the wall.

"I didn't do nothing, Daddy," Malikhi said, giving me the puppy dog eyes that wasn't going to work.

"So, we've learned how to lie now? Go upstairs to your room. I don't like a liar and you're too young to be doing that shit. When I come up there, you better not have a toy in hand or the TV on. I want you to sit and think about why you refuse to listen to your mama."

Malikhi walked to the stairs and lifted his small foot onto the first step. He turned around and opened his mouth. "I don't want to hear it, Khi. Go to your room." My son sobbed all the way to the upper level of our house and I watched him until he got to the top. Jade was cleaning up the toys our son had thrown around the room and I shook my head.

"Bae, Khi is almost three. He's very advanced for his age and you need to start teaching him how to clean after himself. And stop babying his ass too. He thinks everything is a joke and you need to nip that shit in the bud. Fuck being his friend, you his mama and he needs to respect you now!"

"I baby him because he is just that, a baby," she said, slamming toys in the toy box.

Jade was moody as hell and I'd noticed the change when I came back from Atlanta. I wanted to ask her what was wrong but I had a good idea what it could be. Instead of responding to what she said, I walked back into the basement, grabbed a bag and walked back in the room with my wife.

"Come to the bathroom with me."

"I'm not in the mood for your quick sex sessions, Demarius. I'm tired."

"If I wanted to bend you over, it wouldn't happen in a bathroom. This entire house is grounds for you to get fucked," I smirked. "But for real, come here." At that precise moment, the doorbell rang as Jade walked toward the bathroom. "Take this in there and piss on it. Yo' ass too moody around this muthafucka," I said, handing her the Walgreens bag.

The doorbell sounded again and I stalked over because shouldn't nobody be at my shit because I hadn't gotten a call giving nobody permission to come over. Peering through the side window, there were two men in suits standing on my porch and I snatched the door open. It couldn't be anyone other than FBI agents and I'd been waiting on their asses for the longest time.

"Good evening, is Demarius Jones here?" The white one asked.

"I'm Mr. Jones. What can I help you with?"

"I'm Detective Long and this is my partner, Detective Hall. We're from the—"

"FBI," I said, finishing for him. "Come on in. I'm glad y'all finally decided to show up."

Opening the door wider so they could come inside, Jade came out of the bathroom and went straight upstairs with Khi. I was relieved because I didn't need her worrying about what I planned to do once I heard the news these muthafuckas were about to deliver.

"Mr. Jones, we're here to discuss the remains you were inquiring about in Houston."

"Is it being released?" I asked, pulling the blunt from behind my ear. Both of the detectives looked at me with weird expressions. "You can answer the question," I said, lighting the end of my shit.

"Would you mind putting that out?" Detective Long asked.

"Hell yeah, I mind. Y'all don't run shit up in here. When they legalized this shit in Illinois, ain't shit y'all can do to me in the comfort of my own home. Now carry on, nigga." Blowing out the smoke I held in my lungs, I reached over and grabbed the remote to turn on the ventilation system I had put in place for my smoke sessions.

"Yes, the body is ready for release, but you won't be the one to sign for it. See, Mr. Jones, the body isn't your sister's. After further investigation and the autopsy, the charred remains belonged to an African American male. The reason it took so long for the department to get in touch with you is because we just received the results of the dental work. Do you know anyone by the name of William Murphy?"

"No. The name doesn't ring a bell. What do this have to do with my sister?" I asked, leaning my elbows on my knees.

"Mr. Murphy's remains were the only body removed from rubble. His throat was slit and after the autopsy, we were told he was almost decapitated. Your sister wasn't in that explosion, Mr. Jones. Since there's no evidence of her ever being in the house on Maverick Way, we can't declare her dead without a body. Are you sure your sister—" his voice trailed off as he looked through his notebook, "Nicassy was living at the residence?" Detective Hall asked.

"Yeah, I'm sure. Savon should be able to vouch as well." Hearing William was killed was a surprise to me. That meant there was another person involved. This shit was getting more complicated as the days went by.

"Detectives in Houston went to speak with Mr. Cole earlier today. We will be sharing notes tomorrow. Is there anything else you think we should know? Maybe, why all of this happened in the first place?"

"I don't know what the fuck went on in Houston. As you can see, I live in Chicago. The only reason I was in Houston is because of my sister. Don't hesitate to contact me when you have more information about my sister. I want y'all to put this case on your top priority list because if I come back to Houston, the city gon' be the new murder capital. I promise. If there's nothing else, see your way out," I said, dismissing them from my shit.

Both detectives stood and headed for the door. Detective Long turned back and dropped a card on the table. "If any new info come to mind, give me a call."

Nodding my head, I pulled on my blunt and watched them until they were completely out of my house. A lot was going through my mind because I found out where Will was, but Nicassy was nowhere to be found and that shit hit a nerve. I had to call Stone, but first I had to go see if my wife's ass was pregnant again.

Meesha

Chapter 20

Stone

I'd just finished being interrogated by the pigs of the FBI and that shit was exhausting. They were trying their best to pin me to the explosion of my home. I was accused every which way of trying to get money from insurance. When they said I could be looking at up to twenty years in jail, I almost lost my cool. The nigga lying in the morgue was identified as William Murphy. I didn't even know his ass and had no clue as to why his body was inside my house. What's so puzzling about everything was, Angel's body hadn't been found.

Hearing the detectives confirm the body wasn't female took me back to the day I surveyed the damage around my crib. The wheels started turning rapidly in my head and the trap door at Club Onyx flashed before my eyes. The vision made me rush to the guest bedroom and sat in front of my Mac computer.

Tapping away on the keys until I was logged into my surveillance system, I immediately went back to the day my house was destroyed. Someone was in my office and I needed to see who it was. I didn't know why I didn't think about this shit before, but I knew I held a piece to the madness. As I set the recording where I needed it to be, I pressed play and watched. The image was still for the longest time then the closet door opened slowly. I sat up and zoomed in on the screen for it to go black on me.

I hit the rewind button and the same thing happened again. When I fast forwarded the footage, it jumped fifteen minutes ahead. A muthafucka erased my shit. Switching to the cameras on the club's main floor, I searched for any movement and came up empty. I couldn't figure out what happened to save my life. Then it hit me. Angel had access to my system because I needed her to watch the club while I was away on business.

"Her ass is not dead," I mumbled.

"What are you in here talking about?" Sam asked from the doorway.

"I'm just going over some work," I said, logging out of the computer. Telling anyone what I suspect without proof would make me look crazy and desperate for Angel to be alive. "What's up?"

"Shit. I wanted to check on my big brother, is that alright with you? I heard the cops trying to play you like a sucka. They're lucky I didn't come out and pop their asses. I know how to hide a body or two, you know."

"Sam, go sit yo' ass down somewhere," I laughed. "I'm good. I wasn't worried about them muthafuckas. I had nothing to do with that shit."

Standing to my feet, I stretched and ran my hand down my face. I've never been as stressed as I was that day. So much was running through my mind, but I had to put on a façade in front of my sister. The ringing of my phone took my attention and Sam took that as a sign to leave me to handle business. Scony's name was on display as I grabbed my phone from the dresser.

"Talk to me, Scony."

"Did the FBI agents come talk to you yet?" he asked.

"Yeah, them muthafuckas tried to pin this shit on me, but I wasn't going. Obviously, I gave myself a fuckin' concussion and risked my own life. It's the stupidest shit I've ever heard. The body they have isn't Angel's, Scony. It's some nigga named William Murphy. Have you ever heard that name before?"

Scony was quiet for a minute. "Will, is what they called him in Atlanta. He worked for Heat. It's looking as if he was sent to finish the job Nicassy didn't follow through on and never made it out of the house before it blew up. To make matters worse, his ass was killed before the explosion because I was told his head was damn near cut off."

"They didn't mention that to me. He didn't do that shit to himself. That means there was another muthafucka in my shit with him. Now I wonder if Will was trying to stop whomever from killing Angel." Both of us were quiet for a little bit. I knew I was pondering over all I'd learned and wouldn't doubt if Scony was too.

"Those were my exact thoughts. Heat lost some of his good workers; including my sisters because they were inquiring about Will. I think you need to make a trip to Atlanta; it's time for you to meet my sisters. We have shit to figure out. How about tomorrow?"

"I can book a flight now. There's some shit I have to look into." Opening my laptop up for the second time, I went to the airline website and booked a flight quickly. "Scony, I don't think Angel is dead. There's no proof of that, other than her body not being found, but some fishy shit has been going on around my club. That's what I wanted to check out. Hopefully, I'll have some type of information for you when I get to Atlanta. I should be landing about noon, tomorrow afternoon."

"I'm not gon' ask any questions. Be ready to fill me in when I see you and don't leave shit out. We're about to get to the bottom of this shit and too much time has passed already."

"Aight. I'm about to hit the pavement and I'll get up with you tomorrow."

"Bet. Be easy, Stone. See you later." Scony disconnected the call and I sat back before logging out of the computer, grabbed my keys, phone, and headed out the door.

I jumped in my whip and went straight to what was left of my house. The insurance company came out once the property was determined to be condemned. the entire front of the house was destroyed and I didn't know if I wanted to rebuild on the same lot or not. I'd already got in touch with my realtor to find another house and she had sent a few options that I hadn't even glanced at.

Pulling up to the back of the house, I got out of my car and walked through the backyard. From that side of the house, nothing looked wrong with the property. I used my key and entered the sliding door and the damage almost broke me down. There was damage throughout the dining room, living room, and the kitchen. The garage was destroyed along with three of my vehicles, that shit didn't matter to me.

As I scanned the stairs, I needed to get to the second level. There was still a lot of debris blocking my way but I spotted a trail to get through. With each step I took, I prayed the steps didn't give way. I made it to the top as I stepped over parts of the ceiling and went right to the door off the stairs. Opening the door, I smiled because more pieces were coming together.

Lifting the door in the floor, I made sure to lock it from the other side before I descended the stairs. After walking about two miles underground, I came up in my office at Club Onyx. Just as I suspected, Angel got the fuck out of that house. But where the fuck was she? I hoped like hell she would be in the tunnel but she wasn't. As I stood at the door that led outside, I turned the knob and that muthafucka was not locked. My eyebrows furrowed and I walked out and walked down the street looking for any clues I may have found.

"Savon, is that you?" I stopped in my tracks at the sound of the voice.

"Mrs. Linda, what are you doing out here by yourself?"

"I've been walking back here for weeks trying to find you. I heard what happened to you and wanted to make sure you were alright." Mrs. Linda was the First Lady of Missionary Life Baptist Church. She was the mother of the streets and was always looking out for others.

"I'm fine. Thank you for checking on me. I don't want you out here roaming the streets alone," I said, wrapping my arms around her shoulders.

"That wasn't the only thing I wanted to tell you. The young lady you've been courting, she's alright, baby. I know the newscaster said she was presumed dead, but I know for a fact, she's not."

"W—What you say?" I stuttered.

"She's not dead. I found her passed out in the parking lot of the Wendy's down the street the day everything happened. I called for an ambulance and they took her to Jackson Memorial. She was in bad shape, Savon. Go check on your woman."

Thanking Mrs. Linda, I took off running back to my whip. My clothes were drenched by the time I got back to my car. I started the car before getting to it and jumped in and took off. The hospital was fifteen minutes away and I was hauling ass through the streets. There was a car coming out of a parking space and I turned in and made a dash for the door. Inside, I got to the counter and didn't know where to fuckin' begin with finding Angel. Mrs. Linda said she didn't give a name and I was stuck. Taking a chance, I stepped forward nervously.

"Good evening, how may I help you?" the nurse asked with a smile.

"Um, there was a woman brought in by ambulance a few weeks ago."

"That's not giving me much to go on, sir. What's her name?"

"Nicassy White. She was probably brought in as a Jane Doe, because her identification was not on her person when she was brought in."

The nurse tapped away on the keyboard and shook her head in a frustrating manner. Anger was building up, I'd been standing too long for my liking. I scrolled through my phone and a light bulb went off in my head. It was a long shot but I had to give it a try. I found a photo of Nicassy and sat my phone on the counter for the nurse to see.

"This is the woman I'm looking for. Do she look familiar?" I asked, making the picture bigger.

"Oh my God, that's Angel! I remember when she came in that day. She was my patient for the most part." The nurse tapped away on her computer. "She was discharged a few days ago. That's all I can tell you at the moment, sir. But there's a doctor who was assigned to her. He would be able to tell you more on the matter."

"Is he available now?"

"As a matter of fact, he is in the building. I'll page him. You can have a seat while you wait."

I sat in the nearest chair and waited for the doctor to show his face.

It took almost an hour for the doctor to come down and speak with me. I almost left but I needed to hear what happened to Angel. The nurse motioned towards me and the doctor walked across the marble floor in his white lab coat.

"Hello, I'm Dr. Fernandez. What can I help you with?" he asked as I stood and shook his outstretched hand.

"I'm Savon Cole and I need to know about Nicassy White. The nurse said she was discharged under the name Angel White, but I know for a fact, that's not her name."

"Miss White was brought in with a severe head injury and was diagnosed as having retrograde amnesia. It's a type of amnesia where the person is unable to recall events that occurred before the development of the amnesia. Miss White wasn't able to tell us what happened prior to her being brought in, but she was able to remember one person that came in to be with her once she opened her eyes. She was discharged day before yesterday and was advised to follow up with her primary physician."

"Who picked her up?" I asked anxiously.

"Under the patient confidentiality clause, I can't reveal the name of the person she was released to. If it makes you feel any better, she was very familiar with the individual and was pretty happy to leave with him." The doctor stood in wait for my response.

"If anything happens to her, I'll be back to put a bullet in your head. You probably released her to the nigga that tried to kill her!"

I stormed out of the hospital, got in my car and drove to Sam's house to pack. My gut was telling me Angel was in danger and Heat had her back in his good graces.

Meesha

Chapter 21

Layla

Me and my mama had a good day. We went to Five Guys and I had a double cheeseburger, fries, and a vanilla milk shake. It's been a long time since I had fun with my mama. I was glad not to be sad. Being away from Butch was the best times for us other than when she asked questions about my daddy. He always told me what he does in his life ain't my mama's business and I honored that and never spoke on it.

The movie we saw was good. I was finally able to see *Trolls World Tour*. It would've been better if I went to see it with Daddy and Kenzie, but my mama took me instead, since she wouldn't let me go to my dad's house. On our way home, my mama's phone rang and she answered it.

"Hello?" She looked like she was going to cry as she listened to the person on the other end talking. When she hung up, the air in the car became thick because it was so quiet. I didn't know what happened, but my mama was no longer happy. She was driving really fast and that only happened when Butch made her mad. We got to our house and my mama jumped out of the car and headed toward the front door. I got out and slowly walked up the walkway, before she noticed I wasn't with her.

"Hurry up and get in here," she said from the doorway. "Go straight to your room and close the door."

Doing as I was told, I took off my shoes and sat on my bed. I picked up the remote and turned on my TV. I went to the *Disney Plus* app and found the movie *Brave*. Sitting quietly enjoying the movie, the front door opened and slammed shut. I laid back on my bed and cuddled with the teddy bear my daddy bought for me.

"Bitch, what the fuck I tell you about going through my shit?"

Butch and my mama had been arguing every day since she forced me to come back to her house. Butch was nice to me, but when it came to my mama, it was a different story. All they did was scream throughout the house and it was scary. The other day I threatened to call my daddy and Butch told my mama to take my phone. Now, they were cursing again, but there was something different about Butch's voice.

"Who is the bitch you've been texting back and forth, Butch?" my mama screamed.

"None of your fuckin' business! When you seek you shall find what the hell you're looking for. I'm here with your bum ass and you're worried about what the fuck I do on my time. Play yo' role, Tiff, before I put hands on you."

"You talk a lotta shit for a nigga that don't pay bills around here! Tell your hoes to stop calling my phone. As a matter of fact, get out of my house, Butch!"

Hearing them arguing was nothing new. My mama was telling him to get out, but I bet when I woke up, he would still be in the house. I never had to hear the back forth stuff going on when I was at my grandma or my daddy's house. I hated living there. My daddy would come get me… if only I had my phone to call him.

The sound of glass breaking followed by my mama yelling out in pain, my hands started shaking uncontrollably. Butch was beating her up again. Covering my ears to drown out the noise didn't help, because it sounded like Butch was trying to kill her.

"This is what you wanted huh, bitch? You ain't even pay-ing the bills in this muthafucka but you want to try to throw the shit in my face! If it wasn't for your pussy ass baby daddy, you wouldn't have a pot to piss in! Get the fuck up!"

"Let go of my hair! That hurts," my mama cried out.

Slap! A loud thud echoed through my bedroom and I jumped back onto the bed. Creeping to the door, I cracked it open and peered out of the small opening. Butch was cowering over my mama punching her in the face like she was a man. My heart ached for her because blood spewed from her mouth and I think one of her teeth flew across the room. I had to at least try to save her because I was all she had.

Running down the hall in my sock covered feet, I pulled at Butch's shirt, trying to get him away from my mama. "Please don't hit her again, Butch," I cried.

"Go yo' ass back in the room, Layla. This ain't got nothing to do with you!"

My mama kicked him in his stomach and started crawling toward the door. Butch snatch out of the hold my little hands had on his shirt and ran in my mama's direction. When he lifted his foot above her head, I screamed loudly and grabbed one of my golf balls, hitting him on the side of his head.

"Owwwww! You lil muthafucka!" he yelped, bringing his foot down without hurting my mama. "Didn't I tell you to go in the room? I'm about to beat yo' ass for getting into grown folk's business."

I ran to my room, slammed the door and locked it before Butch could get to me. He wiggled the knob as I jumped in my bed praying, he didn't get inside. When he stopped messing with the door, I breathed a sigh of relief. Thinking of a way to call my daddy flooded my mind but I came up empty because there was no way I could get to my mama's room without being seen.

Boom! The door flew open and wood flew to the floor. Butch had kicked his way into my room and I felt the warm feeling of pee flood the bed under me. Just when I thought I was safe, the big bad wolf got in to hurt me.

"You thought I was going to let that shit slide, huh? This is what happens when you try to save a good for nothing bitch!"

The look in Butch's eyes was frightening. I couldn't move a muscle as he walked toward me. He raced over to me and grabbed me out of the bed by my little arm. I felt it pop and suppressed the cry that got stuck in my throat. Looking up, I saw my mama behind him and knew she was going to save me.

She jumped on Butch's back but he never let me go. I was dangling in the air by one arm and it hurt badly. Butch was trying his best to get my mama off him and he succeeded by grabbing the back of her head and flipping her over his shoulder. In the midst of it all, he threw me across the room and my head hit the corner of the nightstand.

Lying motionless on my side, all I heard was my mama calling my name over and over until I fell into a deep sleep.

Chapter 22

Heat

I packed my shit and went to my crib in Snellville. Nobody knew about the property, so it was the best spot for me to lay low. Summer had been calling nonstop and I answered, but every time, she asked where I was. Even after telling her I had business to take care of out of town. Yeah, I should've taken her with me but instead, I made sure all my employees, including Summer were straight before I left. Once I took the money to Will's wife, I hit the highway and got out of dodge.

Rocko called informing of Loco's death and I felt bad because I was the reason for his demise. Loco brought a lot of heat to my establishment but I loved him like a little brother. He had no family and was orphaned at an early age which is the reason I took him under my wing. I made sure he wouldn't lay in the morgue and given a watered-down service because his remains weren't claimed. Rocko handled everything on my behave and had him cremated.

A nurse at Jackson Memorial Hospital in Houston called, explained that she was given my number by one of the patients, and needed me to come identify her. There was only one person who would contact me from Texas and that was Nicassy. I booked a flight and was on the plane three hours later. Now we were in my home in Snellville and the bitch had no idea I was the reason she was laid up in the hospital for weeks.

Keeping the information to myself, I catered to Nicassy and made sure she was okay. A plan formulated in my head and the shit was going to work in my favor. The things I was going to plant in her head may or may not determine if she lived or died. Whether by my hands or Storm's.

"Can we go get something to eat?" Nicassy asked.

"Let me know what you want to eat, I'll order something and go pick it up for you."

"I just want to get out for a little bit. We've been in this house since coming back from the hospital."

It was time for me to put my plan in motion. "Going out is not safe for you, Nicassy. See, there are some folks out there that thinks you are dead. I want to try my best to keep you safe until I can move you away from Georgia so you can start over. In order for me to do that and be comfortable with my decision, you have to be one hundred percent healed."

The look on her face was priceless because she was terrified. Hopefully, the little reveal will make her ass sit the fuck down somewhere. At least until I could convince her to take out Storm's tough ass.

"Why would anyone want to kill me? I haven't done anything to anybody."

"Before you ended up in the hospital, you were a contract killer. You were sent on an assignment to Houston and the target was alerted about your deception. See, you were pretending to love the nigga and Storm tipped him off about your real identity. He blew up his own house with you inside and left you for dead."

Nicassy sat in the chair opposite of me biting her bottom lip. It appeared as if she was trying hard to remember the events I'd told her about. According to the doctor, her memory would start to come back gradually and that was why I had to move quickly with my plan. The last thing I needed was for her to regain her memory and take my ass out. The last conversation I had with her wasn't pleasant and would probably jar her brain pointing the gun back to me.

"Who is this Storm person?"

I was saved by the bell when my phone rang. Glancing down at the screen, it was Summer calling but I didn't care. Long as I didn't have to answer the question Nicassy had asked. "I have to get this. Figure out what you want to eat and I'll place the order after this call." Nicassy left out as I answered the phone and I was glad she did. "What's up?"

"When are you coming back to Atlanta? I miss you, Romero," Summer whined in my ear.

"I don't know when I'll be back, but the minute I do, I'll send you the address to where I am. Summer, if anyone comes by your house asking about me, tell them you haven't talked to me."

"Why would I lie like that? Heat, what the fuck is really going on?" she asked with an attitude.

"The less you know, the better. It's for your safety that you do as I ask. Loco is dead, Will is dead, Tornado dead. Is that shit starting to click in your head yet? Do what the fuck I tell you to do without all of the questions. Now, I have to go and I will see you in a couple days."

Hanging up on her nosy ass, I got up to find Nicassy. She was sitting in the middle of the bed in the guest room with a frown on her face. I didn't need her thinking too hard, so I went to the dresser and got one of the Tylenol 3's the doctor prescribed for her. Grabbing the bottled water from the nightstand, I held both items out to her.

"Here's your medication. Did you figure out what you wanted to eat?" I asked.

"Yeah, I want pizza. Pepperoni and sausage, please."

Nodding my head, I left the room to place her order. My phone rang soon as I hung up from the pizzeria and it was an unknown number. I should've used my better judgement and not answer, but instincts kicked in and I pressed the button to connect the call.

"Who is this?" I sneered into the phone.

"At least I know you're still breathing, nigga. When I get my hands on yo' greedy ass, you gon' wish you had succeeded when you tried to kill me. Buy your family all black everything, pussy; they gon' need that shit."

Stone's threat didn't shake me one bit, but I hurried up and hung up because he was good for tracing shit. Knowing he was moving around made me want to come up with a plan that included his ass too. I was about to shake shit up for everybody involved and they better not underestimate me.

I went into my office, poured a double shot of cognac in a tumbler and tossed it back. Closing my eyes, I allowed my head to fall back against the high back chair. A presence was felt in the room and I slowly opened my eyes. Nicassy was standing in the doorway naked than the day she was born. I'd never looked at her in any way other than she worked for me. Hell, I was digging out the back of her sister for years and here she was throwing the pussy at me. The little voice in my head whispered, "she doesn't know what she's doing. Tap that ass, nigga."

Nicassy lifted one of her breasts to her mouth and flicked the nipple with her snake-like tongue. My dick jumped in my joggers and I reached down to adjust it under the desk. She walked sexily toward me and straddled my lap. I pushed the chair back so she could get comfortable and let her take lead. Nicassy ran her tongue along my ear and traveled down my neck. The wetness from her pussy soaked the front of my pants.

"What are you doing?" I asked stupidly.

"I'm bored, you won't let me go outside, so that means you have to entertain me," she purred.

I didn't have a chance to think about what she'd said because in one swift movement, she was on her knees freeing my joint from its hiding spot. Her tongue glided up the length of my shaft and I let that shit ride. When her warm mouth covered the head of my dick, my breath caught in my throat. Nicassy was now considered the head doctor in my book. She sucked the hell out of my dick and had my toes curling.

Stretching my arm to open the top drawer of my desk, I fumbled around until my fingers touched the foiled package I was looking for. I tore the wrapper open with my teeth and eased my dick out of her mouth. Securing the condom in place, I watched her throw her leg over mine and rode my shit like it was a Mustang. The tightness of her walls had me kneading both of her cheeks between my palms. I met her thrust for thrust as we both came at the same time. Nicassy laid her head on my shoulder and was snoring within minutes. She fucked up because I was going to be sliding into that pussy from here on out.

Meesha

Chapter 23

Phantom

"Eight ball in the corner pocket. Get ready to pay up, Cuz," Khaos laughed as he bent over the pool table with a stick in hand.

"Shut the fuck up and shoot, nigga."

Khaos called to get me away from business that I've dived headfirst into since Layla was taken away from me. I hadn't been out and about since the shootout we had with the Black Kings. Kenzie waited good until I was sleeping to dip out on me and she's back to ignoring my calls and texts. I was cool with it, but I've noticed Kenzie only allowed me to show her affection when she's at her lowest. Fuck that; I'm a grown ass man and don't have time for the childish shit.

Layla had been on my mind a lot and she was the only person I was willing to chase after. My days seemed longer without my daughter, but that's the type of shit life threw at you. Other than making sure my barbershop and carwash was running smoothly, I sat back doing a lot of thinking. Especially, the bullshit Heat left us unknowingly involved in.

"Give me my money!" Khaos' voice brought me back to our game of pool. "A hunnid dollars down, wanna run that shit back? I got time today," he laughed.

"Nah, you got it, fam," I said going into my pocket. I peeled off a bill and tossed it on the table. My mind wasn't into the game and losing my money for fun was something I just didn't do. "You can order some wings and fries though."

"Phan, do I look like Boo-Boo The Fool to you? I'm not paying for shit because I won. Yo' ass lost, you buy, nigga."

My phone vibrated in my pocket and I glared at my cousin as I took it out. Seeing my mom calling had me rushing to answer. "What's going on, Ma?"

"Xavier, I need you at Emory University Hospital."

My mom's voice was shaky and it didn't sit well with me. "Ma, what happened? You okay?" I asked, heading for the exit.

"I'm fine, son, it's not me. Tiffany called—it's Layla, Xavier, get here. I'll be waiting."

When I stepped outside, I glanced around the parking lot for my ride but I didn't see it. Pacing back and forth, I finally said fuck it and started walking until I felt a hand clasp my shoulder. Snatching my hammer from my hip, I turned abruptly aiming the barrel in Khaos' face.

"Whoa, muthafucka! What the fuck is wrong with you?"

"Something happened to Layla. I need to get to Emory now!" I was trying hard not to panic, but it wasn't working out too well for me. My mama said the bare minimum while we were on the phone and that didn't help me any because my mind went straight to the worst case scenario.

"I got you, but my car is back there," Khaos said, pointing behind him. "She's going to be alright, Phan."

"Tiff better hope so," I said storming off.

Practically running into the hospital, I almost raced right past Mama as I headed to the counter. "Xavier!" Stopping at the sound of her voice, I almost broke down seeing the tears building up in her eyes. "Get your visitor passes," she said, pointing to the counter.

Khaos and I obtained our passes and I was ready to make a dash for the elevators. Mama had other plans, because she walked to an isolated section of the lobby and we followed out of curiosity. She stared down at the floor, took a deep breath and started talking.

"Before we go up to Layla's room, I want to fill you in on what happened. Tiff is up there and she is banged up."

"Excuse my language, but fuck Tiff, Ma! What happened to my daughter?" I exclaimed heatedly.

Clearing her voice, my mama told me, "Layla had a severe concussion from hitting her head after she fell. Layla was trying to help Tiff as Butch whooped her ass."

The shit didn't sound believable to me because if she *just fell*, my daughter wouldn't be suffering with a fuckin' concussion. I would learn the truth once my Layla was able to tell me.

"I'm not trying to hear that shit. You can believe that story if you want to, I'm not. There's a lot that wasn't told in the version given. That nigga bet not be up there because I got something for his bitch ass."

The elevator ride was quieter than church during prayer. The only sound that could be heard was me breathing heavily. My heart was beating at a rapid pace and it felt as if I'd worked out for an hour straight without stopping. As the doors opened, my mother grabbed my hand as if I was a toddler and I shook loose and stepped off. The room number on the pass read *517*, and I searched the plates on the wall in search of it.

Chanel was sitting in the hall and I headed in her direction. The question spiraling through my mind was, *how did she know to come here?* Walking down the hall, Chanel lifted her head. Upon seeing me, she dropped her notebook onto the seat beside her and rose to her feet.

"Xavier, Layla is going to be alright. I already called in my report and this is what you needed to get the ball rolling on a case for full custody."

Hearing I could possibly have my daughter back in my custody should've put a smile on my face, but it didn't. I nodded my head at Chanel and pushed the door open to get to

Layla. Tiffany glanced up with swollen eyes and a busted lip. I wanted to finish the job, but I just shook my head at her pathetic ass. There wasn't an ounce of sympathy I was willing to give to her. Instead of saying anything to Tiff, I went straight to the bed and grabbed my baby's hand.

"Come on, baby. Open your eyes for me, Daddy's here," I whispered as I leaned down kissing her forehead.

Pulling up a chair, I held her hand in mine. Layla didn't stir from my touch at all, which was unusual for her. I was the light that brightened her day. Seeing my baby lying in the bed was heart wrenching, it tugged at my heart. Khaos came into the room and placed a purple elephant next to Layla, then kissed her cheek. My cousin stared down at my baby because their bond held them together like Gorilla Glue.

"Phantom, I'm sorry," Tiff said lowly from the other side of the room.

"Keep that shit. I don't have nothing to say to you." A moment later, I changed my mind. "Nah, let me ask you something, Tiff. Is this the end of that nigga kickin' yo' ass?" I asked, turning to face her stupid ass with my arms folded over my chest.

"Butch apologized for what happened yesterday. Layla slipped and fell." Tiff's eyes adverted from mine and I knew she was lying.

"Bitch, did you say *yesterday*?" I asked, standing to my feet. It took everything for me not to approach her and knock her head between the wall and the couch she was sitting on. "Why the fuck I'm hearing about this shit *today*? And why is that muthafucka apologizing? If it was an accident, there's nothing for him to be sorry for. I warned you the day the police came to my mother's house to take my daughter away from me, not to let anything happen to her. I guess you thought I was joking. Tell that nigga I'm gunnin' for his ass. And I'm aiming to kill this time around."

I left out the room because if I hadn't, Tiffany's ass would've been hauled off to the ICU and I would've voluntarily made it real easy for the pigs to escort me to a holding cell. Layla needed me, so all that shit had to be put on the back burner. I had to check my temper, at least until my baby was discharged.

"Xavier," my mama called out to me.

"I'll be back. Go in there and sit with my baby," I shot back as I kept going down the hall.

The doors to the elevator opened soon as I rounded the corner. I didn't hesitate pushing the button for the lobby. Chanel appeared just as the doors were closing and she barely squeezed inside without making the doors open again. Standing in the far corner, I leaned my head against the wall and closed my eyes.

"Xavier, you need to calm down. You were loud as hell in that room and everybody heard what you said."

I ignored the fuck out of Chanel because I already determined what she said on my own. As far as anyone hearing what I said to Tiffany, I didn't care about that shit. It was the main reason I left to be alone, but here she was tagging along like she was invited.

"What happened to Layla—"

"Why are you even here, Chanel?" I asked, interrupting before she could finish her thought. The doors opened and I stepped around her to get out the elevator.

"Karla called and I came fast as I could. You informed her about what we talked about in our meeting and she felt like I should be here to see firsthand what happened to your daughter. I'm just doing my job. Save the attitude for your ignorant ass baby mama, Xavier. Or is it Phantom right now?"

I laughed at her ass while strolling through the lobby. Obviously, Chanel still felt some type of way about the day she willingly allowed me to bless her inner folds with my dick and I left her ass afterwards. I didn't have time for her sensitivity bullshit. Talking about she was doing her job. If that was the case, why the hell was she riding my coattail through the damn hospital?

Making it to the automatic doors, I stepped aside to allow an elderly couple to enter before I made my exit. It was hot as hell outside but that wasn't going to stop me from blowing smoke in the air. I walked a short way down from the door and pulled a blunt from my back pocket. As I touched the tip with fire, Chanel decided to shoot her shot.

"Maybe we can talk about us now, Xavier."

"There is no *us*. We fucked, we came, it's over, end of story. We went over this that day, weren't you listening? What's to talk about?" I asked, pulling on the blunt long and hard.

"When did you become so cold hearted towards me? I know you not still holding Dion over my head."

Blowing smoke out of my nose, I licked my lips, turned my head and spit into the grass. I smiled down at her but she didn't see the humor in my actions. "You the one that brought that nigga up, not me. I didn't give a fuck then, and I could give two fucks now. Hopefully, you didn't leave his ass thinking we would get back together after what we did."

"I love—"

"Phantom!" The sound of Kenzie calling my name paused what Chanel was about to say out of her mouth. I welcomed the interruption because her feelings would've been hurt more than they already were. Kenzie wrapped her arms around my waist the minute she was close enough. "I came soon as I got the call. How's Layla?"

"She has a concussion and hasn't opened her eyes since I've been here. Everybody keeps saying she's going to be alright, but she has to look me in the face before I believe that. I have faith, but it's small at this time." I hugged Kenzie tightly then stepped back a little bit. "Who called you? Let me guess, Khaos."

"Not exactly. He called Kayla to tell her where he was, my sister relayed the message to me."

Kenzie diverted her eyes to Chanel and back at me. I pulled her toward me by the waist, but she moved back slightly. Which caused me to pull her right back where she belonged. The way she stared at me replicated the stance a snake would take before it attacked.

"I'm Chanel—"

"My attorney," I added, cutting Chanel off before she went any further. Chanel would try to throw a monkey wrench into whatever she thought was going on with me and Kenzie. If looks could kill, I'd be a goner. Me interfering in what Chanel was about to say didn't matter. She just had to be the messy one in the situation.

"Like I was saying, I'm Chanel. Who are *you*?" she asked Kenzie nastily.

"For you to be his lawyer, you all in his business. To answer your question though, it ain't yo' muthafuckin' concern who I am. Stick to what he's paying you for, sweetie."

"I am," Chanel smirked. "I get paid in dick payments. That's why I need to know who else is getting it other than myself."

If what Chanel revealed shook Kenzie, she didn't let that shit show. I also knew Kenzie well enough to know she wasn't going to let Chanel think she had one up on her.

"Passing up coins for pipe is stupid on your part. That shit just told me all I needed to know, this nigga don't give a fuck about you," Kenzie laughed. "If he did, you would get the dick and the coins for your services. Don't approach another bitch and say that bullshit like it holds weight." Kenzie laughed and turned to me.

The smile fell from her face fast as hell and what Chanel said pushed her further away from me. "Give Layla a kiss for me. I would go up and see her but I know her trifling ass mama is there with her. Would hate to have to choke that hoe out. I'll see you around, Phantom."

Kenzie walked off, but turned back before she got too far away. "Another thing, find another lawyer because that one gon' get her ass beat if she tries that slick shit again. For the record, find something safe to play with, bitch." She pointed in Chanel's direction before walking off again.

Watching Kenzie until she got in her car, I adjusted my joint in my pants. Whenever Kenzie bossed up like that, my dick jumped around like a fish out of water. I finished my blunt and tossed the roach in the street. Chanel was looking upside my head as if she wanted me to say something to her.

"You're going to fire me because she told you to?" She asked with her hand on her hip.

"Nah, you gon' quit when she fucks you up. That should be the confirmation you need to keep this shit on a business level."

I walked back into the hospital to be with my daughter, leaving Chanel where she stood.

Chapter 24

Scony

Arriving in Atlanta, I had to fight the early morning traffic to Kenzie's house. When I pulled up at her crib, I got out and rang the bell instead of using my key, in case she had company. I had to handle everything I could in this trip because I had to get back to Chicago with Jade. The test I had her take yesterday confirmed my suspicions, she was indeed pregnant again. I was happy and frustrated at the same time because it had become a cycle. Anytime something deep transpired, her ass got knocked up. As if I didn't have enough shit to worry about.

I gave the doorbell another courtesy push because my sister hadn't come to the door as of yet. When I reached in my pocket to retrieve my keys, the door opened slowly. Kenzie stood in a short ass nightgown with sleep in her eyes. Her bonnet was crooked on her head and the mug on her face only made the sight even funnier.

"What the hell are you doing here, Scony? Your phone's not work or something?"

"Are you gon' let me in or what?" I asked, waiting patiently for my little sister to let me in her house. I was trying to do right by her and not barge in like I would in the past.

Kenzie moved to the side and allowed me to enter. I walked to the kitchen and got a bottled water from the fridge as she stood in the doorway with her head leaned against the wall. Gulping half the bottle, I took a deep breath and finished off the rest before throwing the bottle in the recycle bin.

"Scony, answer my question. Why are you back here?"

"I have more information about Nicassy. We can go sit in the living room and talk. Unless you have company, then I'll go in the guest bedroom and get some sleep until later."

"There's no one here except me and Kayla. She stayed the night last night. You want me to go get her?" Kenzie asked as we walked into her living room. Nodding my head yes, she left me alone to go fetch her twin.

Stone had hit me up earlier in the morning and informed me of when he would be landing in Atlanta. I gave him the address to my sister's house and he should've been pulling up any minute. I rested my head back on the couch and closed my eyes. Kenzie and Kayla took their time coming downstairs and it gave me a chance to snooze for a spell. The doorbell rang about ten minutes later, but I was too tired to get up.

"Fuck, this ain't no damn Airbnb, who the fuck told muthafuckas to come to my shit so early in the morning? I'm blaming yo' ass, bro!"

Kenzie fussed from the top of the stairs all the way to the door. I still didn't move, knowing Stone was the only person that could be at the door. My sister hadn't opened the door and I finally sat up and strained my head to see what the holdup was about.

"Bro, come here. There's a man I don't know standing on my porch." I got up and went to the door and opened it without even looking to see what the person looked like. "Aht, Aht! Ask who it is before you let him in here." Kenzie was mad as hell, but I didn't have time to be stalling for time.

"Come on in, Stone. Sorry for having you waiting. This is my sister, Kenzie," I said, walking past her as Stone followed.

We waited for Kayla to join us while Kenzie sat with her legs crossed at the ankles as she glared at Stone. I got up to get another bottle of water and grabbed one for Stone while I was at it. When I returned to the living room, Kayla was coming down the stairs fully dressed; unlike Kenzie who just slipped on a pair of leggings. I was glad they were both ready to hear what I had to say because I needed to fill them in on what I'd learned. Stone had to catch me up on whatever new information he had as well.

"As I said when I first arrived, I'm here because there's new information on Nicassy. I received a call from the medical examiner as well as had a visit from the FBI. Nicassy's body wasn't found in the explosion of Stone's house. The body they found was male and I learned from the detectives that the body belonged to William Murphy."

Kayla and Kenzie had sad expressions on their faces. That was enough confirmation for me to know that William Murphy was in fact, Will. Neither of them said anything right away so I waited until one of them were ready.

"What was Will doing in Houston? This whole scenario isn't making any sense at all," Kayla said, wiping tears from her cheeks. "He would never hurt one of us."

"The way I see it, Heat sent Will to Houston to kill both Stone and Nicassy because she didn't complete the hit. Not holding her end of the bargain automatically put her on the hit list. Will, on the other hand, probably went to Houston to keep Heat at ease but flipped the script when he got there. Whoever his accomplice is, killed Will and left him in the house, and went along with the plan that was put in place. The only difference in the plan was damn near decapitating Will and leaving him to burn in the rubble. Now we need to find out who was with Will the day he died."

"Rocko!" both twins said in unison.

"There's no other person Heat would trust to go out and do anything like that for him. He couldn't ask Phantom nor Khaos because he peeped how close the four of us were. The other young niggas weren't seasoned enough to do it, in

Heat's eyes. Loco was still recovering from Kayla fuckin' his bitch ass up, so he wouldn't have been well enough to carry that shit out. So, my money is on Rocko."

Kenzie broke that shit down, eliminated many and put the bullseye on the target. Rocko surely had his name at the top of the list, right under Heat's. It was time to make some shit shake and I wanted to ride out that same muthafuckin' day.

"Aight, where the fuck can I find Loco, Rocko, and your former boss, Heat?" I asked.

"We have some news of our own," Kayla said, pulling her right leg up on the couch. "Heat supposedly killed a well-known leader of a gang called the Black Kings. He packed up and went into hiding without informing us about what he'd done. The gang got to Loco and murdered him and his girl."

"Loco is scratched off the list but we have bigger fish to fry. The Black Kings came for me and Kayla, but we got away with the help of Phantom, Khaos, and Dreux."

I was madder than a muthafucka hearing that my sisters were in danger behind Heat's bullshit. On top of that, the nigga didn't even forewarn them. His ass better keep running because I better not ever catch his gingerbread-head ass.

"Why the fuck didn't nobody call me about this shit?" I asked looking back and forth between both of them.

"We took care of it, Scony," Kayla had the nerve to say, putting more gasoline on the fire that was inflamed.

"Y'all took care of the muthafuckas that was after y'all that day. What about the rest of them niggas? Don't worry about it. Aye, Stone, get in touch with yo' people and find out all you can on these Black King muthafuckas. They're about to be distinct as of today." I ran my hand down my face as my stress level was at an all-time high.

"What about Rocko? Have y'all found anything on him?" I asked, trying to find out as much as I could.

"No, Rocko and Heat seemed to have vanished into thin air. The club has been closed down and there hasn't been any movement at either house. I was going to hit Phantom up later so he could ride with me to some of the employee's homes to see what we can find out. I also wanted to go question Heat's bitch, but I know she's not going to tell me shit with her jealous ass."

"Leave that hoe to me. I need an address and a picture. I'll work my magic on her and she will be singing like a bird in no time." Stone finally joined the conversation after tapping away on his phone. "I have some troubling news of my own. We may as well get all this shit out in the open."

Taking a sip of water, Stone placed the bottle on the table and turned toward my brother. "I went to the club and noticed the trap door was left unlocked in the closet. I didn't think nothing of it. But learning Angel, I mean Nicassy's, body wasn't found, I did a little digging. I went back to my house and went in through the patio door. I was able to get upstairs to the emergency tunnel I had installed. That tunnel leads to my club, that's a little over two miles from my crib."

Stone had our undivided attention and I kind of thought I knew where he was going with his story. Speaking ahead of time was out of the question, so I sat back and listened with my eyes closed so I wouldn't miss a word. There was going to be some lucrative shit in what he had to say, I could feel it.

"I went through the tunnel to make sure Nicassy hadn't passed out on her way to the other end," Stone continued, before I interrupted him.

"How are you so sure she was in the tunnel?"

"The only person that had access was her. I told her about it in case there was an emergency. There was a set of keys hidden in the back of that closet in case she couldn't get to the ones I had put on her key ring. After surveying the damage of my home, the majority of the damage was in the front of the house. The area of the closet was close to the back and the only damage was the ceiling falling."

What Stone said had me thinking and the shit was very possible. "If she went out through the club, you should have footage, right?" I asked, hoping he would say yes.

"That was my very thought, but when I went to look at the footage, there was fifteen minutes that was erased. I went out the back of the club and the pastor's wife stopped me and told me about finding Angel laid out in the Wendy's parking lot down the street. She told me she called for an ambulance, but she couldn't remember her name to give the paramedics. They did tell her she would be taken to Jackson Memorial."

"We need to head to that hospital! You should've told me this before we flew here, Stone!" I said, jumping to my feet.

Stone was shaking his head no and he must've been out of his damn mind. That was the best news we'd heard about Nicassy yet. But this nigga was basically saying no. It didn't sit well with me and I was ready to blow his shit back because it looked suspect as hell.

"Calm down. I went to the hospital and sure enough, Nicassy was there for weeks. Unfortunately, by the time I got the tip, she had been released. The good news is, she's alive. The bad news is, she has amnesia, Scony. The doctor wouldn't tell me who she left with. Talking about some patient confidentiality bullshit."

"If she has amnesia, how the fuck was she able to remember somebody's number?" Kenzie asked.

"She has a type of amnesia called retrograde amnesia. She won't remember anything leading up to the explosion, but she can remember selective things before the incident. I was wondering why none of you guys were contacted, but some mystery person was."

Sitting back rubbing my temples, a headache was fighting to fuck my focus all the way up. I was happy to know Nicassy was alive, but not knowing where she was ate at my soul. We had to find her.

"Scony, it may not be a coincidence that all of this has come out in the open and Heat just vanished in the wind. It's very possible that he is the one that has Nicassy." Kayla brought up a valid scenario and it was very possible. It actually had me thinking and I was ready to jump on every clue that we had gathered.

"I agree with you on that, sis. But if that's the case, Heat just made shit a lot worse for himself." I leaned to the side and pulled out my phone. When I got the voicemail, I hung up. "Kenzie, where's ya man?"

"What the hell you talking about? I don't have a man. I'm out here solo dolo, bro."

I looked at Kenzie like she had cocaine under her nose. She knew damn well Phantom had her heart in the palm of his hands. Playing a game of lust with a nigga like Phantom, was going to cause her to get hit with love like a ton of bricks.

"You know who the hell I'm talking about. I just called Phantom and his phone went to voicemail. Where is he?"

"I saw him earlier at the hospital. His daughter got hurt trying to protect her mama while she got beat the fuck up by her nigga. Phantom is probably still there with his attorney slash fuck buddy."

Ahhhh, that's what was wrong. Kenzie saw another female in the presence of Phantom and that shit hit a nerve. I understood where the quick comeback came from.

"Who is this nigga that's putting his hands on a woman?" I asked. "It looks like he needs a taste of his own medicine from some real niggas. Especially if his daughter was hurt in the process."

"I don't know much about him. I think if you ask Phantom, he'll tell you all about him. It's the mammy I can't wait to see out in the streets. The last ass whooping I put on her wasn't good enough. And the one Kayla delivered didn't open her eyes either. All I know is, Layla better come out better than she went in that muthafucka, or she will be seeing me on her doorstep."

Phantom ended up calling me back a little while later and me and Stone headed out to fill him in on the latest events. It was about to be a war zone in Atlanta, and there were a lot of muthafuckas on the hit list.

Chapter 25

Phantom

It's been a month since Scony put the buzz in my ear about the connections involving Heat. We searched high and low for that nigga and he still hadn't emerged from the rock he was hiding under. None of the people who worked for Heat knew where he was; at least that was the lie they told. I didn't believe a word of that shit.

We got down on a couple of the members of the Black Kings crew before Brando's lieutenant called for a truce. Dreux told his ass Heat was on his own with the bullshit, but we didn't have a problem clearing the roads of their ass. The way we were laying their men down, I guess the rest of them wanted to keep breathing. For the time being they were straight; unless they decided to renege on what they said.

Layla and I had been having so much fun since she was released from the hospital. It took three days for my baby to open her eyes and smiled at me. I never left her side and had the best alibi when the police came to me with a bullshit lie about me killing Butch. Tiffany sent them my way when she found his bitch ass sprawled out in her front yard with his brains splattered everywhere.

Stone and Scony wasn't playing. They took care of that shit with Butch and kept my hands clean. Both of them wanted to get his ass for what he did to Layla, but mainly because he couldn't keep his hands off a woman. I really didn't give a fuck about him putting his hands on Tiff, it's when he involved my daughter in that shit.

Chanel was trying her best to stay on a professional level with me, it wasn't working for her though. She was able to provide enough evidence for me to get full custody of Layla. Her services were no longer needed, but it didn't stop her from calling my phone multiple times a day. Tiff wasn't feeling that at all because she was granted supervised visitation, every other weekend. I had a phone filled with vile text messages from her and I looked at them and laughed without responding.

"Daddy, somebody's at the door!" Layla's voice snapped me out of my thoughts and I jumped out of my bed and raced downstairs. "Whoever it is been ringing the bell for a long time."

"I'm sorry, baby. Think about what you want to eat while I answer this door."

I opened the door and was surprised to see Kenzie standing on my porch. She had been calling every day to check on Layla, but still hadn't said too much to me. So, to see her standing before me; yeah, I was dumbfounded.

"Hey, can I come in? I have something I wanted to give Layla in person."

Stepping to the side, I waited on her to collect the packages she had sitting on the side of the porch. Kenzie had gifts as if it was Christmas in the summertime. All I could do was shake my head when she handed the bags to me and turned to go back to her truck. She came out with a pink and blue electric scooter. Kenzie bought knee pads, elbow pads, and a helmet to match. Layla didn't need that shit, but who was I to tell her how to spend her money.

"Layla! Where you at, baby girl?" Kenzie hollered as she entered my crib. She pushed the scooter to the middle of the floor and took the other items from my hands and placed them on the couch.

"Kenzie!" Layla said, running from the kitchen right into Kenzie's back. She wrapped her little arms around her waist tightly. "You bought all this for me?"

Her eyes lit up like a Christmas tree and it made my heart pump wildly in my chest. Layla didn't get that excited seeing her own mother, but it was a different story when Kenzie was around. Anyone that didn't know them would think they were mother and daughter when they were together.

"Yes. I thought about my favorite girl when I was out and about today. You are better now and I want you to have fun. I'm going to take you to the park, if it's alright with your father, so you can ride that," Kenzie said, turning Layla around to see the scooter.

"Oh yeah! I like that, Kenzie! Thank you so much!"

"I charged it up and it's ready to go." Kenzie handed Layla one of the bags with a smile on her face. Layla sat on the couch and reached in the bag. She pulled out an iPad and squealed like a pig going to the slaughter house. "That's for when you want to talk to me. Now, you don't have to call from your daddy's phone. My number is already stored. I don't want to hear about you crying about your mama not giving you your phone anymore, you don't need it."

Layla thanked Kenzie again, going back into the bag. My daughter pulled out clothes, shoes, hair bows, barrettes, and a couple of little purses. Kenzie went all out for my daughter and I appreciated it. Layla danced around swinging her gifts. Kenzie's phone rang and she dug in her purse before she missed the call.

"Baby girl, take all of that up to your room," I said, helping her put everything back in the bags.

"Can I go to the park with Kenzie?" Layla was pouting hard to get me to say yes. There was no way I could tell her no after that. "Please, Daddy!"

"Yes, Layla. We can go out to eat after the park. How about that?"

"Yay! Thank you, thank you, thank you. I'm going upstairs to change. I have to be cute to hang out with Kenzie," she said, snatching the bags before running upstairs. "Oh, Kenzie. Would you put my hair in four ponytails?" She paused on the stairs.

Kenzie shook her head yes as she continued her phone call. That was good enough for Layla because she sang all the way to her room.

I do my hair toss
Check my nails
Baby how you feeling?

I had to laugh because her little ass was something else. Long as she was happy, that's all that mattered. I checked out the scooter and I wanted to take it for a spin myself. Glancing up at Kenzie, my joint started getting happy as I looked at the way her ass fitted in her Fabletic leggings. She matched from head to toe in turquoise and black. I zoned out and didn't realize I was caught red-handed, lusting over her thick ass.

"You like what you see, Xavier?" Kenzie smirked.

"I'm not going there with you Kenzie. I won't let you catch me in your web of bullshit today. How are you?"

"I'm good, now that my lil baby is beyond happy. I'm going upstairs to get Layla's hair right. Phantom, when you need her hair done, call me. I don't mind seeing your number, long as it's about Layla."

"You sound like a baby mama and you don't even have kids," I laughed. "Stop the madness. You can act as if you don't fuck with me, Kenzie. I know better, shawty."

"Whatever. I have to hurry because Kayla is going to meet me and Layla at the park down the street from my house."

"Oh, it's just you and Layla riding out, huh?"

"You can come along. Khaos is coming after he finishes whatever he's out doing. That way, you will have someone to keep you out of my face."

Kenzie left the conversation hanging and ran up the stairs two at a time until she was out of my sight. The way the muscles in her legs flexed made me think about the last time them muthafuckas were wrapped around my neck. She knew exactly what she was doing and I had a trick for that ass real soon.

***

We were having a good time in the park talking, smoking, and watching Layla ride the fuck out of her new scooter. Kenzie hooked her hair up in the four ponytails Layla requested, but added a few braids and pink and baby blue ribbons and balls. My baby was cute in her pink capris, baby blue and pink tank and a pair of pink and baby blue high-top Chucks. She looked like a miniature Kenzie riding up and down the bike path.

Khaos had called to see where I was and when I told him I was at the park with the ladies, he said he was on his way. Kenzie kept looking around with a worried expression on her face, which made me glance around myself. I positioned my Glock on my hip just in case.

"What's the matter, Ken?" I asked, walking over where she was standing with Kayla.

"It feels like someone is watching us. Every time I look around, I don't see shit though. Maybe it's just all the shit going on that's bothering me. I'm good, don't worry about it. I'm sure it's nothing." She tried to smile, but it never reached her eyes.

I looked over Kenzie's head to keep an eye on Layla and I saw her making her way back to us. Khaos was walking across the parking lot with something in his hands. I knew damn well he didn't bring nothing for Layla's ass. I didn't think my ears would be able to handle another round of squealing from her. As he got closer, I saw what he had in his arms and I shook my head.

Kenzie saw him approaching, but Kayla's back was turned. Khaos put his finger to his lips indicating to Kenzie not to say anything. In his arms was a white baby pit with a blue collar around his neck. Seeing the dog brought a smile to my face because that lil muthafucka was pretty as fuck.

"Hey, baby," Khaos said, kissing Kayla on the neck when he got close to her. She turned around and her hand went straight to her mouth when she saw the puppy.

"Oh my God! He is so cute!"

Layla heard the excitement and rode her scooter over full throttle. "Uncle K, you bought me a puppy! Thank you, it's so cute," she said, jumping up and down.

I looked at Khaos and the smile he wore a minute ago faded away as he looked down at his lil homie. "Layla, this one isn't for you. It's for Kayla. I'll take you to the pet store to pick out a puppy tomorrow."

"No, the hell you won't! You keeping that muthafucka at yo' crib because it's not coming to my shit."

"But, Daddy!" Layla whined. I gave her the look and even though she shut right the hell up, it didn't stop the tear from sliding down her pretty little face.

"Layla, you can't get everything you see. You ain't never thought about having a dog until now. The answer is no, so clean your face and ride your scooter or we can leave."

"I'm not ready to leave!" She stomped her feet and crossed her arms. I lunged at her and Kenzie scooped her up and walked away. Her little ass was beyond spoiled and I played a major role in that shit, but I would whoop her ass without thought when she got like that. When I said no, I meant it.

"My bad, Cuz. I shouldn't have told her that," Khaos said, handing the puppy to Kayla.

"You don't have to apologize. Layla needs to learn that she can't have every damn thing," I said, rubbing the top of the dog's head. "Is that a blue nose?"

"Hell yeah. When I saw that muthafucka, I had to have it. It reminded me of this feisty, sexy, aggressive female I know." Khaos licked his lips as he gazed at Kayla from the bottom of her feet to the top of her head. She missed the seductive way he bit his bottom lip, because she was checking out the collar around the dog's neck.

"Khaos, why does this damn dog have a diamond tag? That's too much." Kayla held up the puppy and sure enough, the word *Snow* was shining bright in diamonds. When Snow opened his eyes, they were the color of the bluest ocean. That shit called for me to take my phone out to take a pic.

"Nothing but the best for you, queen. I wanted to name him Kane, but that shit was already taken. I don't need him thinking I'm calling his punk ass when I'm actually talking to you."

"He is so beautiful. Thank you, Khaos."

"Get ready, Kayla. Look at his paws, he gon' be a beast. His structure is already forming. How old is this puppy, fam?" I asked as my eyes traveled across the grass where Kenzie and Layla were standing.

Tiffany was stomping on the grass in their direction and I headed that way before anything could transpire. Khaos and Kayla was right behind me, because this bitch wasn't even supposed to be anywhere near my daughter. Tiffany's voice could be heard from the minute she addressed Kenzie as, "Bitch."

"Watch yo' tongue, Tiffany. I would hate to fuck you up in front of your daughter. I'm trying to teach her the right way of life, please don't take it there," Kenzie said, a little too nicely.

"You're not supposed to be teaching her shit! She has a whole mother to do that!"

"I haven't seen you do anything motherly since I've been around. Save that shit for somebody that don't know you in real life. Get out of my face with all that gibberish."

Kenzie grabbed Layla's hand and turned to walk away from Tiff. I started running and scooped her ass up before she could hit Kenzie in the back of her head. Tiff started hitting me in my chest but that shit was nothing to me.

"Why the fuck are you even here, Tiff?" I asked, putting her down once I reached the pavement in the parking lot.

"I want to see my daughter! Seeing y'all shower her with gifts, then seeing y'all in the park like one happy couple is fucked up, Phantom! That's our child and you are letting that bitch play mama to her! I won't stand around and watch that shit happen!"

"Stay yo' ass away from my shit and you wouldn't see anything." I know what I said wasn't making matters any better, but Tiff needed to hear it. "Watching my every move is only going to fuck with yo' head. Stop doing that shit. We will never be a family, Tiff. I have my daughter because you didn't know how to take care of her. Without me providing for her while in your care, she wouldn't have shit. Layla is where she belongs, with me."

"You never cared about me, Xavier. Layla is the only thing you wanted out of our relationship. I've always came second to her spoiled ass!"

Tiffany was showing her true feelings toward my daughter and I didn't like the way it sounded. How the fuck could a mother be jealous of her own child? She was acting like a bitter ex fighting for a spot another woman was able to secure after she fucked up. But she was spitting venom towards her own child.

"Get the fuck away from me, Tiff. It's fucked up how you're talking about my daughter. And you call yourself a mother." I turned and walked away from her and she started calling out to Layla.

"Lay-Lay, come here, baby." Layla stared at Tiffany and walked in the opposite direction to get her scooter. "Fuck all of y'all, including that little bitch you're always protecting. You're gonna wish you never crossed me, Phantom."

Kenzie rushed past me to get to Tiff, but I grabbed her around her waist as Tiff got in her car and drove away. I couldn't let Kenzie beat her ass while my daughter was present. I wasn't going to stop her the next time though. Tiffany was foul for saying fuck my daughter. Saying that shit about me was cool, but my daughter—nah. She violated in the worse way.

"She needs her muthafuckin' ass beat for the shit she said! Don't ever stop me from reaching out to touch her bum ass ever again. That was the perfect time to beat the fuck out of her." Kenzie was mad and I didn't blame her. I had my reason as for why I didn't let her put hands on Tiff and that was Layla.

We walked back to where Layla was and headed back to the truck. Tiff had messed up our outing and I just wanted to get my daughter away from the park. I was putting Layla's scooter in the back of my ride, while Kenzie stood blowing off steam with Kayla and Khaos.

"Layla, get over here, that's still considered a street," I heard Kenzie say to my daughter. I laughed lowly because Tiff was right, Kenzie did fill the role of being Layla's mom.

Lifting my arms to close the back of the truck. The revving of a car caught my attention and I turned abruptly. Layla was taking her time getting out of the middle of the parking lot and my eyes grew wide as I seen the car gunning toward my daughter. I pushed off the truck and made a dash toward Layla. Before I could get to her, Layla tried to run and fell. The back tires caught both of her legs and kept going. My heart plummeted to my feet as I saw my daughter lying on the ground.

"Layla!" I yelled out as I fell to my knees by her side. My baby's legs were positioned in an odd way and I knew they were both broken. The tears flowed down my face as I listened to Khaos on the phone with 911.

"I'm killing that bitch soon as I make sure Layla is okay," I heard Kenzie yell as I hugged my baby.

To Be Continued...
Savage Storms 3
Coming Soon

Submission Guideline

Submit the first three chapters of your completed manuscript to ldpsubmissions@gmail.com, subject line: Your book's title. The manuscript must be in a .doc file and sent as an attachment. Document should be in Times New Roman, double spaced and in size 12 font. Also, provide your synopsis and full contact information. If sending multiple submissions, they must each be in a separate email.

Have a story but no way to send it electronically? You can still submit to LDP/Ca$h Presents. Send in the first three chapters, written or typed, of your completed manuscript to:

LDP: Submissions Dept
Po Box 944
Stockbridge, Ga 30281

DO NOT send original manuscript. Must be a duplicate.

Provide your synopsis and a cover letter containing your full contact information.

Thanks for considering LDP and Ca$h Presents.

Coming Soon from Lock Down Publications/Ca$h Presents

BOW DOWN TO MY GANGSTA
By **Ca$h**
TORN BETWEEN TWO
By **Coffee**
THE STREETS STAINED MY SOUL **II**
By **Marcellus Allen**
BLOOD OF A BOSS **VI**
SHADOWS OF THE GAME II
By **Askari**
LOYAL TO THE GAME **IV**
By **T.J. & Jelissa**
IF LOVING YOU IS WRONG… **III**
By **Jelissa**
TRUE SAVAGE **VIII**
MIDNIGHT CARTEL III
DOPE BOY MAGIC IV
CITY OF KINGZ II
By **Chris Green**
BLAST FOR ME **III**
A SAVAGE DOPEBOY III
CUTTHROAT MAFIA III
DUFFLE BAG CARTEL VI
By **Ghost**
A HUSTLER'S DECEIT III
KILL ZONE **II**

BAE BELONGS TO ME III

A DOPE BOY'S QUEEN III

By **Aryanna**

COKE KINGS V

KING OF THE TRAP II

By **T.J. Edwards**

GORILLAZ IN THE BAY V

3X KRAZY III

De'Kari

THE STREETS ARE CALLING II

Duquie Wilson

KINGPIN KILLAZ IV

STREET KINGS III

PAID IN BLOOD III

CARTEL KILLAZ IV

DOPE GODS III

Hood Rich

SINS OF A HUSTLA II

ASAD

KINGZ OF THE GAME VI

Playa Ray

SLAUGHTER GANG IV

RUTHLESS HEART IV

By Willie Slaughter

THE HEART OF A SAVAGE III

By Jibril Williams

FUK SHYT II

By Blakk Diamond

TRAP QUEEN

By Troublesome

YAYO V

GHOST MOB II

Stilloan Robinson

KINGPIN DREAMS III

By Paper Boi Rari

CREAM II

By Yolanda Moore

SON OF A DOPE FIEND III

By Renta

FOREVER GANGSTA II

GLOCKS ON SATIN SHEETS III

By Adrian Dulan

LOYALTY AIN'T PROMISED III

By Keith Williams

THE PRICE YOU PAY FOR LOVE II

By Destiny Skai

I'M NOTHING WITHOUT HIS LOVE II

SINS OF A THUG II

By Monet Dragun

LIFE OF A SAVAGE IV

MURDA SEASON IV

GANGLAND CARTEL III

CHI'RAQ GANGSTAS III

By **Romell Tukes**

QUIET MONEY IV

THUG LIFE II

EXTENDED CLIP II

By **Trai'Quan**

THE STREETS MADE ME III

By **Larry D. Wright**

IF YOU CROSS ME ONCE II

ANGEL III

By **Anthony Fields**

FRIEND OR FOE III

By **Mimi**

SAVAGE STORMS III

By **Meesha**

BLOOD ON THE MONEY III

By J-Blunt

THE STREETS WILL NEVER CLOSE II

By K'ajji

NIGHTMARES OF A HUSTLA III

By King Dream

THE WIFEY I USED TO BE II

By Nicole Goosby

IN THE ARM OF HIS BOSS

By Jamila

MONEY, MURDER & MEMORIES II

Malik D. Rice

CONCRETE KILLAZ II

By Kingpen

HARD AND RUTHLESS II
By Von Wiley Hall
LEVELS TO THIS SHYT II
By Ah'Million

Available Now

RESTRAINING ORDER **I & II**
By **CA$H & Coffee**
LOVE KNOWS NO BOUNDARIES **I II & III**
By **Coffee**
RAISED AS A GOON I, II, III & IV
BRED BY THE SLUMS I, II, III
BLAST FOR ME I & II
ROTTEN TO THE CORE I II III
A BRONX TALE I, II, III
DUFFLE BAG CARTEL I II III IV V
HEARTLESS GOON I II III IV
A SAVAGE DOPEBOY I II
HEARTLESS GOON I II III
DRUG LORDS I II III

CUTTHROAT MAFIA I II

By **Ghost**

LAY IT DOWN **I & II**

LAST OF A DYING BREED I II

BLOOD STAINS OF A SHOTTA I & II III

By **Jamaica**

LOYAL TO THE GAME I II III

LIFE OF SIN I, II III

By **TJ & Jelissa**

BLOODY COMMAS I & II

SKI MASK CARTEL I II & III

KING OF NEW YORK I II,III IV V

RISE TO POWER I II III

COKE KINGS I II III IV

BORN HEARTLESS I II III IV

KING OF THE TRAP

By **T.J. Edwards**

IF LOVING HIM IS WRONG…I & II

LOVE ME EVEN WHEN IT HURTS I II III

By **Jelissa**

WHEN THE STREETS CLAP BACK I & II III

THE HEART OF A SAVAGE I II

By **Jibril Williams**

A DISTINGUISHED THUG STOLE MY HEART I II & III

LOVE SHOULDN'T HURT I II III IV

RENEGADE BOYS I II III IV

PAID IN KARMA I II III

SAVAGE STORMS I II

By **Meesha**

A GANGSTER'S CODE I &, II III

A GANGSTER'S SYN I II III

THE SAVAGE LIFE I II III

CHAINED TO THE STREETS I II III

BLOOD ON THE MONEY I II

By **J-Blunt**

PUSH IT TO THE LIMIT

By **Bre' Hayes**

BLOOD OF A BOSS **I, II, III, IV, V**

SHADOWS OF THE GAME

By **Askari**

THE STREETS BLEED MURDER **I, II & III**

THE HEART OF A GANGSTA I II& III

By **Jerry Jackson**

CUM FOR ME I II III IV V VI

An **LDP Erotica Collaboration**

BRIDE OF A HUSTLA **I II & II**

THE FETTI GIRLS **I, II& III**

CORRUPTED BY A GANGSTA I, II III, IV

BLINDED BY HIS LOVE

THE PRICE YOU PAY FOR LOVE

DOPE GIRL MAGIC I II III

By **Destiny Skai**

WHEN A GOOD GIRL GOES BAD

By **Adrienne**

THE COST OF LOYALTY I II III

By Kweli

A GANGSTER'S REVENGE **I II III & IV**

THE BOSS MAN'S DAUGHTERS I II III IV V

A SAVAGE LOVE **I & II**

BAE BELONGS TO ME I II

A HUSTLER'S DECEIT I, II, III

WHAT BAD BITCHES DO I, II, III

SOUL OF A MONSTER I II III

KILL ZONE

A DOPE BOY'S QUEEN I II

By **Aryanna**

A KINGPIN'S AMBITON

A KINGPIN'S AMBITION **II**

I MURDER FOR THE DOUGH

By **Ambitious**

TRUE SAVAGE I II III IV V VI VII

DOPE BOY MAGIC I, II, III

MIDNIGHT CARTEL I II

CITY OF KINGZ

By **Chris Green**

A DOPEBOY'S PRAYER

By **Eddie "Wolf" Lee**

THE KING CARTEL **I, II & III**

By **Frank Gresham**

THESE NIGGAS AIN'T LOYAL **I, II & III**

By **Nikki Tee**

GANGSTA SHYT **I II &III**

By **CATO**

THE ULTIMATE BETRAYAL

By **Phoenix**

BOSS'N UP **I , II & III**

By **Royal Nicole**

I LOVE YOU TO DEATH

By Destiny J

I RIDE FOR MY HITTA

I STILL RIDE FOR MY HITTA

By **Misty Holt**

LOVE & CHASIN' PAPER

By **Qay Crockett**

TO DIE IN VAIN

SINS OF A HUSTLA

By **ASAD**

BROOKLYN HUSTLAZ

By **Boogsy Morina**

BROOKLYN ON LOCK I & II

By **Sonovia**

GANGSTA CITY

By **Teddy Duke**

A DRUG KING AND HIS DIAMOND I & II III

A DOPEMAN'S RICHES

HER MAN, MINE'S TOO I, II

CASH MONEY HO'S

THE WIFEY I USED TO BE

By Nicole Goosby

TRAPHOUSE KING **I II & III**

KINGPIN KILLAZ I II III

STREET KINGS I II

PAID IN BLOOD **I II**

CARTEL KILLAZ I II III

DOPE GODS I II

By **Hood Rich**

LIPSTICK KILLAH **I, II, III**

CRIME OF PASSION I II & III

FRIEND OR FOE I II

By **Mimi**

STEADY MOBBN' **I, II, III**

THE STREETS STAINED MY SOUL

By **Marcellus Allen**

WHO SHOT YA **I, II, III**

SON OF A DOPE FIEND I II

Renta

GORILLAZ IN THE BAY **I II III IV**

TEARS OF A GANGSTA I II

3X KRAZY I II

DE'KARI

TRIGGADALE I II III

Elijah R. Freeman

GOD BLESS THE TRAPPERS I, II, III

THESE SCANDALOUS STREETS I, II, III

FEAR MY GANGSTA I, II, III IV, V

Meesha

THESE STREETS DON'T LOVE NOBODY I, II
BURY ME A G I, II, III, IV, V
A GANGSTA'S EMPIRE I, II, III, IV
THE DOPEMAN'S BODYGAURD I II
THE REALEST KILLAZ I II III
Tranay Adams
THE STREETS ARE CALLING
Duquie Wilson
MARRIED TO A BOSS... I II III
By Destiny Skai & Chris Green
KINGZ OF THE GAME I II III IV V
Playa Ray
SLAUGHTER GANG I II III
RUTHLESS HEART I II III
By Willie Slaughter
FUK SHYT
By Blakk Diamond
DON'T F#CK WITH MY HEART I II
By Linnea
ADDICTED TO THE DRAMA I II III
IN THE ARM OF HIS BOSS II
By Jamila
YAYO I II III IV
A SHOOTER'S AMBITION I II
By S. Allen
TRAP GOD I II III
By Troublesome

224

FOREVER GANGSTA

GLOCKS ON SATIN SHEETS I II

By Adrian Dulan

TOE TAGZ I II III

LEVELS TO THIS SHYT

By Ah'Million

KINGPIN DREAMS I II

By Paper Boi Rari

CONFESSIONS OF A GANGSTA I II III

By Nicholas Lock

I'M NOTHING WITHOUT HIS LOVE

SINS OF A THUG

By Monet Dragun

CAUGHT UP IN THE LIFE I II III

By Robert Baptiste

NEW TO MONEY, MURDER & MEMORIES

THE GAME I II III

By **Malik D. Rice**

LIFE OF A SAVAGE I II III

A GANGSTA'S QUR'AN I II III

MURDA SEASON I II III

GANGLAND CARTEL I II

CHI'RAQ GANGSTAS I II

By **Romell Tukes**

LOYALTY AIN'T PROMISED I II

By Keith Williams

QUIET MONEY I II III

THUG LIFE

EXTENDED CLIP

By **Trai'Quan**

THE STREETS MADE ME I II

By **Larry D. Wright**

THE ULTIMATE SACRIFICE I, II, III, IV, V, VI

KHADIFI

IF YOU CROSS ME ONCE

ANGEL I II

By **Anthony Fields**

THE LIFE OF A HOOD STAR

By Ca$h & Rashia Wilson

THE STREETS WILL NEVER CLOSE

By K'ajji

CREAM

By Yolanda Moore

NIGHTMARES OF A HUSTLA I II

By King Dream

CONCRETE KILLAZ

By Kingpen

HARD AND RUTHLESS

By Von Wiley Hall

GHOST MOB II

Stilloan Robinson

<u>BOOKS BY LDP'S CEO, CA$H</u>

<u>TRUST IN NO MAN</u>
<u>TRUST IN NO MAN 2</u>
<u>TRUST IN NO MAN 3</u>
<u>BONDED BY BLOOD</u>
<u>SHORTY GOT A THUG</u>
<u>THUGS CRY</u>
<u>THUGS CRY 2</u>
<u>THUGS CRY 3</u>
<u>TRUST NO BITCH</u>
<u>TRUST NO BITCH 2</u>
<u>TRUST NO BITCH 3</u>
<u>TIL MY CASKET DROPS</u>
<u>RESTRAINING ORDER</u>
<u>RESTRAINING ORDER 2</u>
<u>IN LOVE WITH A CONVICT</u>
<u>LIFE OF A HOOD STAR</u>

Meesha